KNOX

INTERGALACTIC DATING AGENCY

DRAGON BRIDES
BOOK EIGHT

KATE RUDOLPH

ABOUT KNOX

A wannabe reformed **thief and a dragon lord looking for love...**

After witnessing the skills of the Intergalactic Dating Agency at finding mates, Knox enlists their services to find a woman of his own. He's collected a hoard of precious stones from across the galaxy, a mate will be his crown jewel. But is he looking for love, or another treasure for his collection?

Fresh off a prison colony, Aria wants to go straight. But when her past catches up to her, her only choice to escape a gnarly fate is to infiltrate Knox's home and steal a gigantic diamond right from under his nose. She's got the perfect cover: the Intergalactic Dating Agency.

But as she gets closer to the fiery dragon lord,

the last thing she wants to do is betray him as he rouses feelings in her she never knew she could feel. When Knox finds out the truth, will he help her or will the betrayal be too much to overcome?

How can she keep her dragon mate and escape her past?

CHAPTER ONE

"I'M SORRY, but the position has been filled," the diminutive, bright pink alien chirped at Aria when she showed up for her interview. She glanced at the blinking HELP WANTED sign and then back at the alien, but the alien just kept smiling.

No luck.

"Do you know of anyone else that's hiring?" Aria asked. They were on a space station, the kind of place that was always busy and always looking for people willing to stick around to work demanding jobs for little pay. Aria was willing. She had to be.

She could still feel the phantom weight of the prison collar she'd worn for the last year and a half. There was no lasting mark, but her skin felt permanently chafed with the imprint of it. She wasn't going back to a prison colony. Her old life was over, now she had to make something new.

The pink alien made a face. "Not with your... work... history. Now please leave, I have customers to see to." There were no customers waiting in the small makeup store, but Aria didn't argue.

Damn it!

Finding fake papers was hard when she didn't have the money to do it. What accounts hadn't been seized by the stinking authorities who'd caught her had been looted by forces unknown. It turned out there wasn't any honor among thieves. And that meant that Aria was forced to live under her own name, the one she'd been given by the heartless little orphanage on Hephastia Prime that was full of cast-off children with no past and no future.

She'd heard that some of the shops on this station wouldn't care that she had a criminal record and had done time for theft. She was beginning to suspect the places willing to hire her were the bars on brothels on the lower decks, provided that she let them amp up her less than ample bosom and agreed to the kind of work she'd have to do on her back.

Aria would avoid the mods for now. She still had a few credits to her name and she was more than a little cunning. Not every kid back at the orphanage could have made it more than a decade before getting locked up in a prison colony. And Aria had only been caught because some rat turned snitch.

She found a seat at the edge of the food court and slumped down, allowing exactly three minutes for moping. She could afford another night in the dingy room she'd rented, but after that she'd need to vacate and find a free corner to sleep in until she had steady money coming in.

How did people do it? She'd been trying to make an honest living for two months and it felt like her skin was being stripped off of her in tiny strips. So far she'd been eking by with small jobs fetching and carrying for the ships that were passing through, but the work was highly competitive and unsteady. Not to mention the captains were happy to stiff anyone not smart enough to get payment up front. And captains knew that paying up front ran the risk of getting scammed out of the work.

No one could trust anyone in this damned place.

An alien with strange antennae coming out of his green head stood up, a flashing device clutched in his pincers indicating that his food was ready at one of the vendors. He left a bulging black bag on the table and Aria sat up straighter.

All she had to do was stand up, hook her arm

through the strap, and keep walking like she hadn't done anything wrong. The alien wasn't paying attention, no one else was looking at her, and the lift would be so easy that a child could do it.

Hell, if she were training a child, it would be the perfect test.

But Aria forced herself to stay still. She wasn't doing that anymore. She didn't need to be a thief to survive. She could develop skills, earn an honest living. Everything in her rebelled at the idea of going back to prison, and she couldn't risk it for a mystery bag.

She felt the barest brush of something at her own hip and her hand lashed out, latching onto a tiny wrist and the small person who yelped when she tightened her grip.

Aria glared at the young human girl who couldn't have been older than thirteen. She had the desperate look of an urchin, but a cunning glint in her eyes. This wasn't her first attempted lift.

"Go hunt someone else, little one." Aria had enough compassion not to call for the guards, even if a small part of her wondered if that might end up better for the girl. Aria could remember what it was like to be fourteen years old and unceremoniously ejected from an overcrowded and underfunded orphanage.

"Ragnar wants to see you," the girl said. "Follow me."

Ah. So the girl had already landed in a powerful orbit. And Aria could feel herself being pulled along.

She forgot about the defenseless bag on the table beside her and followed the girl. Truthfully, Aria should have expected something like this to happen, for her old life to come calling. Forced as she was to live under her own name, it wasn't like she could hide.

But she'd thought Ragnar, at least, might let her go. All debts between them were long paid, and she hadn't said a word about his crew while she faced down the tribunal that decided her fate.

The girl dropped her off at the door to a small booth hidden away along a hallway of the space station. They could be rented to make calls or do work, or just to snatch a bit of privacy in the busy place.

The door slid open, and Aria took a seat while the girl ran off.

Ragnar was a decade or so older than Aria. He had his finger on the pulse of the biggest scores in this quadrant of the galaxy and always got away clean. Prison was for other people.

He smiled when he saw her, his bushy beard crinkling. His eyes were small and dark, unreadable, and his smile certainly didn't reach them. He kept his hands on the table, framing a folder.

He was trying to appear nonthreatening. That couldn't be good.

"I hear you got out a few months ago," he said, voice low and raspy, as if something had damaged his throat. He'd sounded like that for as long as she'd known him.

Aria shrugged. Ragnar wasn't the most violent man she knew, but she was locked in a tiny room with him without backup. The booths were sound-proofed enough so that no one would hear her scream. Not that she expected it from Ragnar, but she'd felt the sting of his palm a time or two, and she didn't want to chance it.

"Thought you might have come looking for work," he said. He tapped a finger on the cover of the folder.

"I'm done with that now." She kept her gaze on him, refusing to glance at the folder. Whatever was in it was a gateway to her old life. Sure, the payout would be good, but at what price? It was never just one job with Ragnar.

Once he got his hooks into a person, he didn't let go.

And here she was, hooked again.

"Ari, baby, you're one of the best I've ever seen. You're in your prime, you can't quit." His smile turned beseeching, as if this was just a conversation between old friends.

"I'm not going back to prison, and this is the way to stay out. I didn't say a word while I was inside. I didn't contact anyone. As far as I'm concerned, it's all forgotten, okay? Whatever you're planning, you should find someone else." It would have been the perfect moment to slide out of the booth and leave, but there was no doubt in her mind that Ragnar was controlling the lock on the door. She was stuck in here until he let her go.

"You worked for a long time. I'm surprised you're in a place like this. Didn't you always say you'd buy an estate on Sigma Epsilon?" He wasn't smiling now. No, it had turned into a knowing grin.

The bastard. Now Aria knew exactly what had happened to her money. "You raided my accounts? Really?"

He shrugged. "Not like you were using it. And I

was keeping it safe for you. I haven't touched a single credit."

She clenched her jaw and had to take a deep breath before she started showing any more emotion. Any reaction she gave him would only work against her. "Thanks for looking out for my money, Ragnar, but I'd like it back now."

"Of course." He slid the folder her way. "But I need you to do a job for me first. Then it's all yours and we're square."

Aria didn't flip it open. "I'm out. I haven't lifted a single thing in nearly two years. My contact list has gone cold and I don't have any supplies. I'm not the person you need for this job."

"Normally I'd agree. But I've been laying the groundwork on this one for a while and it's finally paying off. What do you know about the Intergalactic Dating Agency?"

"What do mail order brides have to do with anything? I don't do sweetheart scams." She could run a grift as well as anyone, but love cons got dirty fast.

"Open the folder, Aria. You're not saying no to this one."

She laid her hand over the top of the folder, but didn't open it. "What if I do?"

He splayed his hands wide and shrugged. "The Imperium is still looking for who pulled off the Nali heist."

"I was a hundred light years away from the Imperium when that happened. I don't touch those jobs." The Imperium didn't imprison low level thieves. They executed them. Slowly and painfully. The only hope of mercy came from offering information that an influential Imperium family could use against their enemies.

"And I have travel documents that show you were within a few hours of Imperium space both before and after the job, along with an account holding enough credits to suggest a Nali-sized payoff. Do you really think their bounty hunters will stop to ask questions?" He nodded to the folder. "But there's no need for that. Just take a look. This job won't even take a week. And then you'll have your money back and we'll be done."

There was no escaping Ragnar. Even if this job went well and he let her walk away, he'd be back with a similar threat. If Aria was a little stronger she might have been able to say no and walk away. There had to be a hole somewhere deep enough to keep her hidden from the Imperium.

But that life would be even drearier than the existence she was trying to eke out here.

And if she had her credits back, she wouldn't need to prostrate herself by selling low quality makeup to commuters who didn't give a damn.

She flipped open the folder and gave a low whistle when she read the stats on the diamond she was about to poach.

Lord Knox of Vemion wouldn't know what hit him.

CHAPTER TWO

Dɪᴅ he like the black tunic with the silver threading or the red one with the intricate bird embroidered on his back?

Knox studied himself in the mirror, brow furrowed as he considered the possibilities. What did each outfit say about him? Would his date think he was staid and conventional if he wore the black? Was he outlandish and free-spirited if he wore the red? And since when did he care about clothes? Yes, his closet could clothe a whole party of the king's favorites, but normally Knox cared about his clothes for their function, not their sartorial impression.

He shrugged out of the red tunic and slipped into the black. This was a first impression. Simple was best.

A burst of laughter came from the door in the corner of his room. Knox's gaze snapped to where his brother, Flint, stood in the doorway, arms crossed and head thrown back in mirth. "If Asher could see you now, brother." He gasped it out between bursts of laughter.

Asher was their other triplet, off to journey the galaxy with his newly discovered mate. That discovery had prompted Knox on this quest of his own, and thanks to the IDA, he would have a chance at finding what his sibling had.

Maybe.

"I heard you put in an application, too," Knox said as he straightened the buttons of the plain shirt under the tunic. "Too lonely on your sleek little spaceship?"

Flint made a rude gesture before stepping into the bedroom and flopping down onto Knox's bed, heedless of the clothes Knox had already discarded. "Did you see the new model of the Starcross Racer? I'll have one delivered before year's end. And if you're lucky, maybe I'll let you borrow my old Starcross for your honeymoon."

Knox threw a hanger at him. "Let's not get ahead of ourselves. I haven't even met the woman yet."

"You asked a dating agency full of psychics to

find you a mate, I hardly think I'm getting ahead of myself. Stars above, you're boring." He picked up the red tunic and held it out to Knox. "Wear this one so you can trick her into thinking you have a personality."

Knox glared, but he snatched the tunic out of Flint's hand and switched outfits. "Is this insane? I've never cared about finding a mate before."

"If you want to blame anyone, blame Asher. But he's so damned happy that I don't think he'll care. I didn't realize he could smile after so many years on that blasted rock." Flint shuddered.

"Remy's still there," Knox reminded him. Their youngest sister had taken over Asher's role as administrator of a colony in the process of being terraformed. She reveled in the power.

"Remy will rule Vemion if the king isn't careful," Flint joked. They were all in line for the throne, technically, but at last count there were at least seventy people between Knox and power, and he didn't wish any of them ill, at least not ill to the point of death. He didn't want to be a king; dragon lord was more than enough for him. "So who is this woman you're meeting?"

Knox nodded to a small printout on his dressing table. "Her name is Aria, she's human, though not from Earth. My contact at the agency said it's not standard procedure to give too much information about potential matches. They don't want people coming in with preconceived notions. We're having dinner by the river. Her flight is supposed to be getting in soon." And he'd be running late if he kept talking. "The red, you think?" He tweaked his collar and turned around to give Flint the best look.

His brother had a considering look on his face. "You'll never be as handsome as me, but I think you'll do."

"Right. Are you staying in the townhouse?" Flint had an estate on the other side of the country, and when he came to the city, he stayed with Knox. Knox didn't mind. The place was too big for him alone.

"I'm taking a test flight of a prototype racer," Flint said. "I'll be back sometime next week."

"How safe is this prototype?" Flint liked speed and danger, and he'd had more than one close call. Knox wanted to say more, but if he was too heavy handed, he'd push his brother away. Flint was an adult, and Knox didn't want him resenting the relationship they shared.

Flint grinned, sharp and toothy. "Safe enough, don't worry."

Knox waved and left his brother to his own

devices. He could worry, but he'd learned long ago that it was useless. His brother would do what he wanted and nothing could stop him.

Knox left Flint and headed downtown on foot. He was close to the center of the city, to all the action of the capital, and he liked it that way. The restaurant he'd chosen for this first date was a particular favorite. The food was divine, but the atmosphere wasn't overwhelming.

He was a bit early and ordered a bottle of wine. He hadn't received word that Aria's ship was delayed, but he wasn't sure he would. Would the IDA get in touch if something happened? Surely yes.

As the clock ticked by, he began to wonder. Five minutes late turned into fifteen. At thirty minutes, he pulled out his communicator to contact his IDA handler and ask what was going on. He received no answer.

Hmm.

He waited another thirty minutes, wondering if there was some mix up of time zones and trying to give Aria grace. But after an hour and a half, he'd had enough. He paid for the wine and left the restaurant, calling the IDA again and leaving another message.

This wasn't a good first impression. How was he supposed to find his mate if she stood him up?

He took the long way home, wanting to clear his head in case Flint was still there. His brother wouldn't let him hear the end of it. Knox didn't normally have problems with women, so this would no doubt earn hysterical laughter.

The streets of his neighborhood were nearly empty in the early evening. As he got closer to his house, he saw a figure sitting slumped over on his stoop, shoulders heaving.

Knox approached slowly. "Excuse me, is something wrong?"

The woman sucked in a shuddering breath and looked up at him, big eyes glimmering with tears. She wiped at her face and swallowed, throat bobbing. "I'm so sorry, I had nowhere else to go. Can you help me?"

It was Aria, his date.

CHAPTER THREE

THEY ALWAYS FELL for the crying act. Every guy, deep down, wanted to be a hero and save the damsel. All playing the damsel gave Aria was a headache, but she hoped it would lead to riches.

Or at least it would start her on the path to dig herself out of the hole she was in.

If she ever got the chance, she was going to *end* Ragnar.

She breathed deep and let out another heaving sob, ignoring the way it made her temples throb. "Everything's ruined," she said through her tears.

Knox, the hapless mark, hovered over her, one hand suspended just above her shoulder as if he wasn't sure that he should touch her or not. Aria wanted to tilt her head up and get a good look at him, to see if the picture she'd seen really did him justice. Instead she kept her head down. She had to sell this. She wasn't sure just how sharp this Knox guy was, and she wasn't going to fail before she started.

"My bags were stolen," she wailed. "My communicator, my credits, everything! That damned captain kicked me off the ship with nothing. This is the only place I could think to go."

"How did you know where I live?" Knox asked. He sounded curious, not suspicious. Good.

Aria wiped at her eyes and sniffed before looking up. Stars, he was gorgeous. Tall and broad, with a strong jaw and piercing eyes. There was a faint pattern to his skin, almost as if he was covered in small scales, marking him as a dragon shifter. But what really caught her eye was the bright red tunic.

It was certainly a statement.

"I asked the directory bot at the space port." That had the added benefit of being true. Knox's address wasn't hidden, and he lived in the center of the city. Easy pickings. "I'm so sorry, I should go. This was a mistake." She sniffed and looked around, as if she had a bag she could pick up and take with her, before she slumped her shoulders, as if remembering that she was empty handed.

"Wait." Knox finally put his hand on her shoulder and gave it a comforting squeeze. "You must be hungry. Come inside and we'll figure this out."

Yes! She clamped her lips together to keep from smiling. She was supposed to be dejected, not triumphant.

The entryway of Knox's townhouse was opulent and befitting a dragon lord. It was a large space, with high ceilings and ornate decorations that bordered on gaudy but were no doubt expensive. Their footsteps echoed from the marble floors, a white tile threaded through with veins of gold and black with speckles of something greenish.

But it was just an entryway. A servant seemed to materialize out of nowhere—or possibly from the discreet servants' passage door disguised in the paneling of the wall—and took Knox's shoes once he slipped them off. The servant gave Aria a considering look, but Knox waved him off and guided her further into the house.

"Would you like a drink?" he asked once he'd led her into a small sitting room off the front hallway, the large window looking out onto the city street.

"Just water, I guess." In another lifetime she might have asked for a stiff drink. But she wasn't about to dull her senses at the beginning of a job. As for coping... she'd figure that part out later.

Another servant, this one a woman with bright red hair ruthlessly tamed in a braid, appeared a few minutes later with a pitcher of water, two glasses, and a plate of meats, cheeses, bread, and fruit.

Knox closed the door behind the servant before taking a seat on the couch. "Now, tell me what happened."

Aria took a deep breath, as if she was gathering the courage to speak. She hated this. She didn't do the long con, not anymore. And Knox seemed nice, damn it. This one was going to mess her up.

She plowed on. "It's like I told you. I arrived on Vemion for our meeting after the IDA set up my transportation. The captain was... not good, and I was eager to get off his ship. But when I tried to leave, he told me there was an extra fee and that I could either give him three hundred credits or pay... another way." She shuddered. This story wasn't real, but Aria had met plenty of creeps in her life, and this one *could* have been.

A wisp of smoke curled behind Knox's ear and his eyes flashed. Her research into dragon shifters told her they sometimes let off smoke if they felt strongly.

The story was working.

She felt like an asshole.

"What was his name? His ship's identification?" he demanded, rising from his seat and striding across the room as if he could take down the evil captain on his own.

She shook her head. "We docked near the cargo ships rather than the passenger port. I had all of the ship's information in my IDA documents but... well, I think his name might have started with an R. I'm sorry."

He turned to her, clutching the back of her chair. "This is not your fault. But why didn't you just meet me at the restaurant?"

She huffed out a frustrated laugh. "I couldn't remember the name. All I knew was that your name was Knox and I had to find you."

He made a noise in the back of his throat, and she knew she had him. The big bad dragon lord would protect her.

And she would take him for all she could.

His fingers brushed against her arm as he stood once more. "I need to go make a call and get a meal for us. Just stay here, please."

There was nowhere else she'd rather be. But Aria just nodded meekly. Once he was out of the room, she reached forward and plucked a chunk of cheese off the plate and scarfed it down. Then she took a look around the room. Apparently no one had ever told Knox it was a bit gauche to flaunt wealth. The walls were decorated with original paintings set in gilt frames.

There were cases lining the walls with every-thing from statuary to lesser gems on display. If she just stripped this room of what she could carry in her pockets, she'd be set for months.

But a small sapphire necklace wasn't what Ragnar wanted.

"Have you heard of Nafari sapphires?" Knox entered the room so quietly that Aria nearly jumped in fright. But it wasn't illegal to admire sapphires in a case, and Knox didn't know why she was really here.

She shook her head and Knox was off, explaining the special mines on Nafar and the mineral content that gave the stones a strange inner light she hadn't noticed before. Aria found herself stepping closer to the case to admire it, not because it would be easy to steal, but because it was beautiful.

"You're an emerald," Knox said once he was done explaining the sapphires.

"I am? Why?" Aria didn't own gems. She stole

what she needed and passed them on for credits. She didn't have the space to keep pretty things. And that had probably saved her from a longer sentence on the prison colony.

No space to think of that now.

Knox stepped close, eyes flicking up and down. "Your coloring, to start with. You should wear green. And your eyes." Their gazes locked and Aria's stupid stomach decided to clench, not in fear but in—no, she couldn't desire the mark. "You would shine in emeralds."

Now might be the time to casually inquire about the diamond, or at least steer the conversation that way. If she played this right, she could be out by tomorrow evening. But she kept her mouth shut. There was no use appearing too eager.

"I'm having a servant prepare a room for you tonight. We can contact the IDA tomorrow and see what we should do."

"You really don't have to do that," she demurred.

"Consider this our official date," he insisted. "We were supposed to meet anyway. Let me help you."

Aria let herself smile. "Alright. Thank you, Lord Knox."

"Just Knox, please."

She leaned in and kissed his cheek. "Got it."

Out of the corner of her eye, she saw a discreet camera tucked inside one of the decorations on the wall. She'd need to figure out this place's security before she made her next step.

She let Knox lead her into the dining room, mind whirring with possibilities.

CHAPTER FOUR

Aria was trouble, Knox knew it deep down in his bones. A woman like that didn't just show up on his doorstep, crying her big eyes out, and begging for help. Knox wasn't immune to her charms. There was something magnetic about the way she'd thrown herself at him, all vulnerability and desperation. That had never attracted him before, but with Aria...

She wasn't telling the truth, at least not the whole truth. He wasn't certain what to do about the woman staying in the guest room—he wasn't about to kick her out, but he needed to find out more about her.

And he wanted her, oh how he wanted her, even if he shouldn't.

Though why shouldn't he? The Intergalactic Dating Agency thought they made a good match.

If she really *was* his match. He knew from his own brother's experience that the agency could find a man his mate. But what if the woman staying in his guest room had stolen the true Aria's identity?

If she had, this woman knew exactly how to approach him. And how to look. Stars above, his body ached for her, the kind of yearning that had his cock hardening with every thought. Why did she do this to him? All he wanted was something simple, a woman to stand at his side, a woman he could keep.

Flint had accused him of wanting another pretty bauble to add to his hoard. But was that so bad? He was a dragon, after all.

And if he wanted answers, he knew exactly where to start.

The roof of his townhouse was a simple place, strewn with light colored stone and with a small area off to one side with a few chairs and a table for socializing. But the only reason Knox came up here most of the time was for convenience. He took a running start and launched himself off the edge of the building, shifting to his other form and spiraling between two townhouses on the other side of his street.

He pumped his wings hard, gaining altitude until he was so high the stars were visible even with the lights of the city below. He flew towards his older brother Soren's house.

Soren and his family lived at the far edge of the city, in a smaller estate on a beautiful property. He landed with a soft thump on the crushed gravel path in the courtyard.

The night felt like it had gone on forever, but the sun had barely set and Knox had a moment to worry he'd come at the wrong time. Soren had a young child and a wife who expected his full participation in their lives, even with his busy job as a captain of the city guard. But Knox had only walked halfway up the path to the sandstone house when Soren's tall form slipped out the back door. He nodded towards the pergola in the back where a wide bench sat amongst the statues.

Knox followed him and took a seat. He tapped his fingers against his leg, restless energy thrumming in him. Flying only made his blood race, and the concerns that Aria's presence brought up made it worse. He wanted to pace, but he forced himself to remain sitting. All would be well, he just had to make it through this.

"You haven't been here in a while," Soren said,

taking his own seat. He pulled a golden cigarette holder out of his breast pocket and flicked it open, offering Knox a clove cigarette. Knox declined, and Soren took one for himself with a shrug, lighting it with a snap of flame from his fingers before putting the case back in his pocket. "When I said you're invited to family dinner, I meant it. Even Asher brought his girl around a few weeks back."

"And how did that go?" Asher's mate, Zoe, was a wonderful woman, and Knox was glad for his brother, but the full force of their family would be hard for anyone.

"You know Mom," Soren said, sucking on the cigarette. "Already asking about grandchildren."

That Knox could believe. "It's not about dinner, it's about—" He sighed and rubbed a hand over his face, trying to make things make sense in his own head. "Something's up."

Soren blew smoke out of his nose and watched it trail upwards. "Yeah?"

"You know I met with the IDA?" Knox asked. He hadn't told his parents, of course. His mother happily demanded babies from all her progeny, and he wanted to put it off as long as possible. But nothing happened in the city that Soren didn't know about, or at least that was how it always seemed to Knox.

His brother nodded. "And how was it?"

"She stood me up and then showed up crying on my doorstep, claiming a nefarious captain had robbed her of everything after demanding sexual payment." He told the rest of it slowly, unraveling the knot as best he could. "I want to believe her, but it seems too..." He wasn't sure of the word.

"You think she's lying?" Soren flicked some of the ash from his cigarette and took another drag.

"Maybe." It came out far more anguished than it should have been on an hour's acquaintance. "And I don't want her to be a liar." The admission felt like it was pulled from deep in his soul.

"Do you want me to look into her? Check her flight manifests and run a check on her credentials? What does the IDA say?"

"Yes." Knox could hire his own people, but why would he when his brother had access to resources he'd never have? "As for the IDA, no one answered tonight, but I'll try again in the morning. I don't want to jump to conclusions, but I want to know I'm doing the right thing."

"Your instincts are good, kid. Trust them." There was a childish yell from the house, and Soren sighed and snubbed out the cigarette. "Duty calls. Do you want to come in and say hi?"

Knox gave his brother a brief hug. "Not tonight. Not until I know whether I've let a snake into my house."

Soren returned it with a pat on his back. "Goodnight, then." He stubbed his cigarette out and headed back inside.

Knox flew back home quickly, even though the breeze was delightful against his scales and he could have flown for hours. He landed on the roof and half expected to find most of his belongings gone when he returned. But all seemed to be where it belonged. If Aria was there under false pretenses, she had a specific goal, rather than robbing him blind.

His housekeeper greeted him with a smile. "Your guest has retired to her room, my lord. She's been there since you left. I believe she ran a bath not too long ago, and I took the liberty of sending up extra towels and a bedtime snack."

"Thank you. That's all for tonight." Instead of going to his own suite, he headed to his office and pulled up the security feed. It felt like spying, which, Knox supposed, it was, but he'd be foolish not to check. It only took a few minutes to confirm that his housekeeper was correct. Aria had been in her room the entire time since he'd left.

So why didn't that satisfy him?

Did he want her to be here under false pretenses? Did he crave some sort of intrigue? He slumped in his chair and wished he'd had the foresight to grab the whiskey. He forwarded the file he had from the IDA with Aria's photograph and other details to Soren and hoped that would be enough to solve the mystery.

He didn't want Aria to be some assassin, or spy, or master thief. She was just a woman, he hoped. A woman who might be exactly who he was looking for.

And that felt too easy.

Ah. There it was.

He'd filled his house, his life, with beautiful things, gems from across the galaxy, artifacts from long dead civilizations, things that no one else could have. But it was the joy of hunting them down, of acquiring them, that truly spoke to Knox. He didn't just think 'I'd like a large diamond' and make an order. He searched out the rarest and the best, and he did his damnedest to acquire them. He didn't want something delivered to order.

Including a wife.

As he stood to head to his own suite, he had a vague thought that he should put Aria up in a hotel or have her stay with his older sister, Nix, rather than staying in his home. But if she was settled into her room for now, he wouldn't bother her. All could be decided in the morning.

He took the long way to his quarters, passing by her room and pausing to listen for any hint that she was inside, but it was quiet. It should have been, he'd paid a good deal for soundproofing.

A part of him was tempted to knock, to see if Aria might invite him inside. But if her story checked out, then she was a traumatized woman, and there was no space for fantasy. If the story didn't check out, she was a liar and he couldn't get involved.

But as he settled into his own quarters, body frustrated with want, all he could wonder was... what if?

CHAPTER FIVE

Knox held out a hand to Aria. "Take it, come on!" he yelled over the sound of engines firing somewhere behind them.

Aria strained to reach him, but it was too far. Then something seemed to grow out of his back, impossibly long and large and covered in thin skin and scales. A wing.

That was when she knew she was dreaming.

Still, she grabbed onto the wing and he yanked her close, the wing disappearing as they ran for all they were worth. "I've got you," he promised. "Here, you'll be safe." He shoved her through a door that seemed to appear by magic, and then they were in a bedroom.

No, not just any bedroom. It was the sumptuous

guest room she was currently sleeping in. Knox backed her up against the wall and covered her mouth with his own. Heat flooded her and her body responded instantly, and she couldn't suppress her moan. She arched up against him and dug her fingers into his back, trying to pull him closer.

He tasted like fire and cinnamon, hot and spicy and delicious. One of his hands tangled in her hair and the other went to the waistband of her leggings, yanking them down while his tongue pressed into her mouth, insistent and demanding. She parted her legs to allow him better access and he made quick work of his own clothes, his impressive length pressing up against her stomach.

"Fuck," he muttered when he broke the kiss. He yanked her hair to tip her head back and the motion made heat bloom deep in her belly. She'd always liked it a bit rough, and her dream-Knox knew it. He reached down and cupped her ass, lifting her off the ground. She wrapped her legs around his hips, shuddering as his cock pressed against her.

Then her eyes snapped open.

Aria groaned, body hot with need and tight with frustration. The sheets were curled around her legs, and one boob was hanging out of the tank top she'd worn to sleep. She curled her hands into fists and held tight, willing her body to calm down.

She wasn't about to get herself off in the mark's house, in a bed the mark owned, while thinking about the mark's thick cock.

Her core pulsed and she gritted her teeth.

Damned inconvenient attraction. It had been a long time since she'd wanted anyone, and she didn't think anyone had ever lit her up like this, especially not so quickly.

She was going to punch Ragnar the next time she saw him for getting her into this mess.

I've got you, you'll be safe.

Knox's words from the dream echoed in her head, and that was enough to get her out of bed. Self-delusion had no place in a job like this.

She washed up and opened the wardrobe to see what clothes she'd been provided. She wished she had her own things, but this con required her to come in empty handed. Well, mostly empty handed.

She'd released a small mapping bot after Knox had shooed her to her room. It looked a bit like a spider, with long spindly legs and a dark, plump body, and right now it was crawling through the house and searching for the diamond along with scanning for any obvious security measures. It would flag cameras and keypads, but if he had booby traps or other counter measures, she'd have to be on her toes. The bot was so tiny that it would take at least a day or more to map the house, so she'd be patient.

The wardrobe had a handful of outfits, all of them simple and possibly taken from one of the servants. At least it wasn't a uniform. Aria still had nightmares of what she'd been forced to wear in the prison colony.

She pulled out a simple tunic and leggings and gave the fabric a feel. Unless his servants were paid exceptionally well, this didn't come from them, it was too expensive. A sister, maybe, or a lover.

A sudden pang of jealousy stabbed at her gut, and Aria glared at the leggings as if they'd burned her.

This job was going to be the end of her.

Though she hadn't worn them the night before, Aria pulled on a pair of glasses she'd been keeping in her pocket. She didn't need them for her vision, but the bot was attached to them and she could call up the incomplete map it had already made simply by adjusting one of the arms of her glasses. She needed Knox to get used to seeing her in the glasses so he didn't question them.

But Knox wasn't the person she saw when she finally went down to the dining room for breakfast, spine steeled against the too-sexy dragon's appeal.

A four year old girl in pigtails sat at the head of the table, munching on fluffy pancakes. She smiled brightly when she saw Aria. "Hi! I'm Mazy."

Knox wasn't supposed to have a kid. It wasn't in the file, and she didn't do jobs where little ones could get hurt, not if she could help it.

Ragnar's deserved punch had just been upgraded to a kick.

In the balls.

"Hi, Mazy. Where's your dad?" Aria didn't deal with a lot of kids, and she wasn't sure how she was supposed to talk to one so young.

Mazy chomped on her pancakes and spoke with a full mouth. "He's talking to Uncle Knox. I think it's about Mommy's birthday. They're being sneaky."

Uncle. The relief that washed over her was definitely disproportionate.

She fixed herself a breakfast plate from the food that was set up on a sideboard and sat at the table, leaving a chair open between her and Mazy. Before she could think of anything else to say to the kid, a man who might have been a few years older than Knox walked in. He smiled when he saw the pancakes in front of Mazy, and the resemblance between him and Knox was obvious.

Mazy's dad.

And a cop.

It was the same everywhere, the way he held himself, stiff shoulders, eyes darting around the room for any threat, the slight bulge under his jacket where a weapon probably rested. He gave Aria a polite nod and she offered a suspicious smile, slipping right back into character. Aria the Victim wouldn't be smiling brightly at strangers, she'd be wary. And she wanted this guy gone.

"I'm Soren," the cop told her. "And I see you've met Mazy. We just came over for breakfast. I'm Knox's older brother."

"Aria," she said, grabbing for her coffee, sipping it before he could offer a hand.

"Yeah, Knox let me know what's going on." Soren's smile didn't slip, but there was unease in his eyes. He didn't trust her.

And neither did Knox.

It was a strange relief. If Knox bought it fully, it meant he was an idiot. Of course, that made her job much easier, but she didn't like the thought of him being stupid. And no one had the kind of collection that Knox did without some level of competence.

It made the job harder, in theory. But she'd robbed smart people before. And intelligence made them predictable. He'd have security cameras and keypads, a decent system to keep his valuables where they belonged. But she wouldn't need to worry about the things that people who only *thought* they were smart relied on.

She shuddered, remembering a laser shooting droid that had nearly killed her on one of her early jobs. It had been easy to disable once she got close, but she still had a scar on her leg from where a lucky shot had skimmed her.

"You ready to get out of here, kiddo?" Soren asked, holding his arms out for Mazy.

The little girl got out of her seat and ignored her father's outstretched arms. "Okay, but I can fly myself, daddy."

Right, 'cause the kid was a dragon. What kind of trouble did baby dragons get up to?

"Let's say bye to Uncle Knox first. Say bye to Miss Aria, too." Soren nodded at her.

Mazy waved, and Aria waved back. She was relieved once the child and the cop were gone, but she couldn't let her guard down. She jiggled the arm of her glasses and looked at the map of Knox's house overlaid on her regular vision.

Nowhere near complete. If she could stay another day, she'd have the map, and once the bot found the diamond, she'd be ready. Then she'd be gone. She just had to keep Knox on his toes and keep the cop-brother from finding her out.

Easy.

Knox walked in a few moments later, his expression serious. He poured himself a cup of coffee and joined her at the table, looking like he was about to deliver bad news. "Soren is looking into that captain of yours. He's in the city guards, has good connections. We'll do what we can to recover your things."

Was that really why he had the cop looking into her? She couldn't ask.

"And I contacted the IDA," he continued. "They need to know they can't rely on that ship. Hopefully we can get this sorted out shortly." This news was fine, so why did he look so haunted?

He was going to send her away.

The certainty of it washed over her. And Aria couldn't have that, not with the bot scouring the house. She just needed another day. "Thank you so much," she said before he could speak again. "You've done so much for me already, you didn't need to look into the captain. Really, I probably brought it all on myself. You know how guys can't—anyway. I can be out of your hair soon. My mom is on Aquila, and if you let me set up a relay, I'm sure she'll wire me the funds to get me passage back to her."

There was no such mother and nothing but an answering service on Aquila, but it was on the other side of the galaxy, and messages took nearly a day to travel that distance. It would buy her the time she needed to do her work.

Some of the tension leeched out of her dragon, and he offered her a small smile. "No need to hurry," he told her. "But I can set up the relay for you. And you're welcome here. I have plenty of room."

"Thank you!" She was tempted to hug him, but that might be overselling it.

If she touched him, she wasn't sure she could deny the lust.

"And since we didn't have our date last night, what do you think of a visit to the park today? After all, the IDA put us together. We should see if we're the match they think we are." He offered it with a hopeful smile.

Aria's heart clenched. She wasn't supposed to get involved. She could play this off, pretend she was too horrified by her journey here and hide in her room. Doing that might even help her finish the job faster.

But apparently her mouth and her brain weren't in agreement, because she found herself speaking. "Yeah, I think I'd like that."

Staying close to Knox would only make things more complicated. But, for some reason, she couldn't help herself.

CHAPTER SIX

KNOX WAS MORE and more certain by the moment that Aria wasn't what she seemed to be. Her story was too convenient. Soren hadn't been able to chase down anything about the supposed criminal captain. And Knox still hadn't heard a word from the IDA.

His only choice was to keep her close. He was protecting his hoard, nothing more.

She didn't seem dangerous. Then again, the most dangerous creatures wrapped themselves in a web of deceit to draw their prey closer. And there was no doubting that he wanted as close as he could get.

Her green eyes captivated him. There was intelligence there, but also fear and vulnerability. For some reason, Knox wanted to comfort her. Wanted to slay whatever beast she faced and to become the beast that kept her safe, always. She'd be the crowning jewel of his hoard. If he could figure out the truth.

"Do you really want to go to a park?" She blinked those eyes at him and adjusted her glasses.

"If you're willing." It was early yet, but Knox was eager to greet the day, and keeping her out of the house would give Soren the opportunity to run more in depth security scans without Aria noticing. He had the best systems that were available on the planet, but it was a big galaxy out there and there were always tricks to get by the best locks.

She bit her lip and glanced down before smiling up at him. "I'm very willing."

The words went right to his cock, and Knox had to grip the edge of his seat to keep from reacting. There was a lovely blush to her cheeks that said she knew exactly what she was doing. Vixen.

Women rarely tempted him the way that things did. They were too unpredictable, with no place in his orderly life. Once or twice, he'd made attempts to build a relationship, but when he went haring off on his next search, his would-be love always somehow got left behind. Would it be the same with Aria?

Perhaps he wasn't cut out for a mate.

With that dreary thought, Knox left to get ready for their outing. He changed into casual clothes and slipped on his wrist communicator. Soren would message him when it was clear to return.

He sat on the bench in the entryway of the house and scanned through his messages while he waited for Aria. Several minutes had passed, and he wondered if this was another test. Before he could wonder further, he heard footsteps at the top of the stairs and looked up. And stared.

Stars above.

Aria wore a dress the color of summer grass. It clung to her body and revealed enough to make his mouth water. The fabric of the skirt swayed as she walked towards him and Knox rose, swallowing hard. He wanted to clutch her waist, to run his hand over the bare skin of her collar until she arched against him. He wanted to bend her over the couch and press inside her, to mark her as his own and hear her cry his name in pleasure.

It was one hell of a dress.

Aria smiled brightly at him and twirled around. "I found this in the wardrobe. What do you think? Is it your sister's?" She grabbed the skirt and held it out, swaying from side to side.

Unable to stop himself, Knox settled a hand on her waist, holding it there until she stopped moving. She tipped her head up to look at him, their eyes locking. The smile slid off her face, replaced by something darker, something hot. Her tongue darted out to lick her lips. Then she closed her eyes and angled her face away.

"It's lovely." Knox forced himself to drop his hand and back up a step. He had no right to touch her so freely, no matter how badly he wanted it.

The look on her face, the way her pupils had dilated... he wasn't alone in this. Whatever had brought her to him, she wasn't faking her reaction. No one was that good.

Aria wrung her hands together and looked around the hall as if for an escape. Knox cleared his throat and offered her his hand. "Ready to go?"

Her slender fingers slid over his own, the soft skin making him suppress a shiver. He squeezed gently and tugged her forward, out the door, and onto the street. He guided her down the small, clean alley between his house and the next. It led to the gated garden shared by the houses on the street. If he had his own estate, his grounds would dwarf this shared space, but it was enough for him.

For now. Maybe one day his mate would want more.

"Is this all yours?" Aria asked, awe in her voice, as they stepped onto the pebbled path and began to walk between the towering trees.

"No, not all of it," he answered, nodding with a smile towards a family playing at the far side of the park, two dragonlings bobbing in the air as they learned to fly, their parents in their human forms watching. "But I can access it any time I want."

"That's... really nice." There was a note of melancholy in her tone. "Not too long ago..." She trailed off and shook her head.

"What?" He wanted to know more, and her tone now was so different than before that it had a ring of truth to it.

"For a while I was... in a place that didn't have much greenery. I would have done just about anything to have a spot like this." She reached out and ran her fingers over the bark of a nearby tree.

What he wouldn't give to be the tree.

"What made you contact the IDA?" he asked. This was supposed to be their proper first date, he reminded himself.

She shrugged. "I guess it was time. What about you? You have all this." She splayed her arms wide and spun around at his side, keeping graceful pace with him. "Surely you could have anyone you want." She glanced at the family on the far side of the park just as the mother of the dragonlings tossed a ball of flame in the air to the delight of the children, who flew circles around it. "Can you do that?"

"I fly much better than small children," he assured her.

She snorted and then covered her mouth and nose, eyes wide. "Sorry. But no, the fire. Is that why you need an off-world bride? Are you shooting blanks?"

"Excuse me?" But he laughed while he said it, the mirth startled out of him.

"What?" Her expression was open, her smile wide.

The urge to kiss it roared up again and he quashed it.

Knox summoned his flame, the ball as big as his head as he bounced it between his hands. "No blanks here, my lady." He let the flame roar up in a geyser before summoning it back into himself like it had never been there. He reached out to tuck a stray strand of hair behind Aria's ear, letting his fingers trail over her cheek as he dropped his hand back to his side. "I'm a healthy young dragon in my prime."

Her breath stuttered, and her eyes drifted closed. "I'll keep that in mind."

It finally felt like he was seeing the real her, and Knox wanted more. But before he could suggest anything else, perhaps a trip to the city or even an offer to take her flying on his back, his comm vibrated on his wrist, and he flinched.

"Is something wrong?" she asked.

He glanced at the screen. Soren. "I have to take this. It will just be a moment." She nodded and he stepped off the path while she meandered a little ways down, looking at the trees.

He engaged the call, a holographic projection of Soren floating above his wrist. "Security has been reinforced," his brother said.

"Anything else?" The privacy module built into the device ensured his caller couldn't be overheard, but that didn't mean that a person—Aria—standing nearby couldn't hear him speaking.

"Nothing. Your housekeeper gave me the woman's dirty clothes before they were washed and I scanned them for anything suspicious, but the chemical and radiation readings are all in line with what I'd expect after a relatively long space journey.

I dug a little deeper into the alleged captain, too. Yesterday a ship whose captain's had more than one complaint of disorderly conduct and harassment landed just long enough to refuel and drop off a small load of cargo. He goes by the name of Raweliond. Cargo ships like his sometimes take passengers from smaller ports. They report it through the cargo port master, but it can take a bit of time to sync into the main immigration system."

Something like relief pooled in Knox's belly. "So her story might check out."

Soren shrugged. "Looks like it does for now. But I saw the way she looked at me this morning."

"How?" A flicker of something like jealousy flared.

"Like a criminal looking at a city guard."

"You *are* a city guard," Knox had to point out. "Anyone can spot it on you."

"Don't get blinded by your cock," his brother warned. "I don't like this."

He wasn't cock-blind. "Thank you for the work," he told his brother before disengaging the call.

He looked over at Aria and smiled. She was crouched at the base of a tree, her hands cupping something. Her face had grown serious and he wondered if something was wrong. But some force made him hold back. She was holding a small, chirpy bird, he realized. One that had fallen from a nest high above her head.

Aria pursed her lips as she studied the bird and then studied the tree. Knox was tempted to head over and offer to help, and he would. In a moment. If she needed it.

She held the bird close and said something to it before sliding the bird into one of the pockets on the side of her skirt. Then she took a deep breath and leapt for the lowest branch, which was several centimeters above her arm's reach. She made it and pulled herself up with surprising arm strength, hoisting herself up on top of the branch, careful not to disturb her pocket.

Knox was done watching. She was high up, and if she fell, he was going to catch her.

"Oh, um, hi!" Aria glanced down, clearly not afraid of the height. "One second." She reached into her pocket and scooped up the bird, carefully reaching for a nest on the next branch and placing the chirping creature into it. "All good. I just... um... wanted a better look."

"You're rescuing a baby bird." It came out like an accusation.

"What? No!" she sputtered. She turned towards

him and her footing slipped. She let out a curse, but there wasn't enough branch for her to regain her footing. She held up her hands, trying to steady herself, but that only made things worse and she tipped, her foot catching on another branch that snapped under her weight. She let out a sharp gasp as she started to fall.

Knox lunged forward, his hands outstretched and arms waiting. She landed on him with a crash, sending him plunging to his knees.

"Shit." She grabbed at his shirt, tugging herself closer for a moment. "Thanks for catching me."

"Anytime." He held her tightly, unable to make himself let her go. The position was awkward. It couldn't be comfortable for her. But she wasn't moving away either.

Aria shifted, and suddenly she was sprawled on top of him. Knox fell back, his hand going to her waist to keep her in place. "You're safe," he muttered, staring up into her eyes.

Her pupils had dilated again, the desire evident, and her breath had sped up. "Yeah," she said. He ran a hand up and down her back, and she leaned closer.

There was no denying the inevitable.

Knox captured her mouth with his own. Aria let out a little sound of surprise and then moaned against him. She melted into him, one hand tangling in his hair. Their tongues brushed against each other and Knox growled low in his throat. His grip tightened for only a moment. This was madness, the kind he could lose himself in forever.

"Joniss!" one of the adult dragons from across the park yelled.

Knox smelled burning wood and pulled back, looking up to see one of the branches—safely clear of bird's nests—smoldering, and one of the dragonlings bumbling in the air only a few feet away.

The dragonling bumbled back, as if he hadn't nearly burned the two of them, and Knox sat up, helping Aria to her feet.

The taste of Aria lingered on his lips for the rest of the morning.

CHAPTER SEVEN

THIS WAS why Aria hated the grift. Jobs like this got a girl too close to the mark, and the guilt that assailed her couldn't be washed away with any number of credits. Knox was *nice*. And sexy. And so damned perfect that he made her want to scream.

She didn't want to rob him. She wanted to climb in his lap and ride him for the rest of her life.

Emotions were stupid.

He was gone now, at least. Their walk, that kiss, it was all she could take for one morning, and when they'd arrived back at the townhouse, she'd claimed to have a headache and retreated to her room. When she'd dared to venture out an hour later, there hadn't been any sign of her dragon lord.

Which was a good thing, she reminded herself.

She wanted unfettered access to his house, not to *him*.

A light on the feed in her glasses was blinking, and Aria nudged the arm to pull off the map.

Done.

Her bot had found the vault, predictably fortified in the basement. The lock looked intimidating, but she didn't worry since she wouldn't be dealing with it.

Knox was smart. He was cautious. That meant the vault was likely fitted with standard safety measures, including a panic button. If her spider bot could get inside and trigger it, the door would open like the lock didn't exist. Unfortunately, it would also most likely send an alert to the proper authorities and any private security Knox employed, but she could deal with that.

She just had to wait for her moment.

It wasn't now.

Ideally he needed to be gone from the house. She'd need a speedy getaway vehicle and a ride off the planet. The second the vault unlocked, Knox would know it was her and he'd be betrayed. But Aria shoved that thought aside. Hurt feelings weren't why that mattered. She'd be flagged at every port on the planet.

Hopefully Ragnar would come through on his end of the deal. He'd given her the bot and promised she'd have a ride off the planet once she gave him the signal. He wanted the diamond enough that she was pretty sure he'd come through.

Though he'd try and screw her over. Somehow.

She'd have to worry about that part later.

Knox's office was one floor below her bedroom, and Aria walked down the hall, pretending to look for a sitting room that looked out over the park. If anyone spotted her, she'd claim to be turned around. She was keenly aware of the cameras in the hallways and forced herself to keep a pleasant smile on her face as if she wasn't snooping and trying to sneak into his lordship's office.

The door was locked.

Of course. Smart, cautious, annoying man. It was almost like he didn't trust her.

"Can I help you, miss?" a servant carrying a folded pile of towels asked her.

Aria smiled at her. "Is this the sitting room? Lord Knox said I could find it here." He'd said no such thing, of course, but who cared?

"Sorry, miss," said the servant. "That's one floor below. That's his lordship's office." There was a note of censure in her voice.

"Oh no!" Aria clutched a hand to her heart. "I must have misheard." She made a face. "I'm so sorry. I guess that's why the door's locked. Downstairs, you said?"

"Yes, miss. I can show you." The servant hesitated, clutching the towels.

Aria waved her off. "No worries. I've got it now. This place is so big!"

"It is, indeed, miss."

Foiled. It had been a long shot anyway, but Aria had to try. With the cameras on her and the servant sure to make a report, Aria headed down to the sitting room and flopped onto a couch, putting her feet on a footrest and crumpling.

She didn't want to do this. Knox had been nice to her. He was a good man. And, sure, he had far too much money for any one person, but she couldn't hold that against him.

She wanted to walk away. But she remembered the dank smell of her cell in prison, the way the bugs crawled over her in the night, and rats scampering over her body as if she wasn't there.

Bile rose in her throat and Aria clutched her legs close to her, curled in a ball as if that would protect her from the dark memory of those terrible months.

The Imperium would put that prison colony to

shame. Torture. Cells filled with bugs and rodents on purpose, rather than out of neglect. And then a slow, painful death for a crime she hadn't committed.

"Are you alright?" Knox's voice startled her.

Aria realized a tear had escaped and quickly wiped her cheeks. "I'm fine. Just a bit... overwhelmed by it all—oh!" she looked up at him and nearly bit her tongue. His tight shirt clung to sweat soaked skin, and his pants seemed painted on, giving her imagination a lot to work with. He looked carved from marble and brought to life by sensual magic.

She wanted to lick him.

"I just finished my workout." He stretched his hands into the air and rolled his head from side to side. "Everything alright?"

"Definitely fine," she forced out. "No more headache. I was just admiring the view." Her cheeks flamed and she stammered. "Of the park. The view of the park."

His lips twitched and he lowered his arms, flexing. She noticed. Of course she did. That's why he was doing it. Then his expression grew serious. "I could show you a thing or two. In case you run into another unscrupulous captain. How to get out of a grab. I have a sparring room." He nodded back towards the door he'd come through.

Aria had changed out of the sexy green dress once they were back from the park and now wore a tunic and leggings. She didn't tell Knox that she knew how to punch a guy.

If Knox wanted to get up close and personal...

She wasn't supposed to be doing this. She should turn him down and start putting space between them. This was only going to hurt them both when she got into his vault.

She stood up and nodded. "I could use a lesson or two." And maybe she'd show him a surprise of her own.

Knox's sparring room was exactly what a rich guy who liked the newest tech would have. There was a programmable sparring bot charging on the wall, and the floor was made of a squishy material that wouldn't hurt too much if they went to the floor. There was a punching bag in one corner, and various training weapons hung on the wall. "The rest of the gym is through there," Knox said, and pointed to another door. "There are more workout machines, if you'd like to use them."

Aria just nodded, a lump in her throat.

She wasn't supposed to be doing this. It was wrong.

So why couldn't she stop?

"Show me what you got, Mr. Lord." She had to force a bit of cheer into her voice, but once Knox stepped close, the guilt flared for a moment and then fled. All she could see, all she could think about, was him.

She was in so much trouble.

"Let's just start with a simple grab," he said, wrapping his fingers loosely around her wrist. Everywhere his fingers touched was electric. Aria sucked in a thick breath.

"You're going to want to grab onto my hand and try to peel my fingers back," Knox instructed, keeping his fingers on her wrist. "Then give me a shove."

It was a move she could do in her sleep, though she'd found it never really worked when an asshole had a firm grip. She was more likely to give him a swift kick where it hurt and hope it did the job. But Knox let her go and smiled when she did it correctly.

"That's good. Really good."

The praise washed over her, making her shiver. But his eyes darkened as he watched her reaction, and this time the hand that closed around her wrist was firm.

She tried to pull free. But he didn't let go.

"Let's try something else." There was a huskiness to his voice that made her throb.

He dragged her along with him, his grip unbreakable, until he had her pressed up against the wall, his body too close for comfort. Or it would have been, if it wasn't him. He leaned over her, his lips only a breath away. She wanted to take her free hand and wrap it around his neck, to pull him close, but the look in his eyes stopped her.

"What would you do if I had you backed against the wall?" he asked.

She licked her lips and arched up on her toes. "This." She brought her knee up, aiming for his center. But he twisted his hips to the side, and somehow flipped her, dragging her to the ground. He ended up on top of her, her wrist still clutched in his hand, but now it was clamped to the ground over her head.

He straddled her waist, knees pinning her on either side. "What now?" he demanded.

It made her shiver. "I'd never let a man get me to the ground like this." It was all bravado, and more than a little shaky. She was powerless under him and a small—and possibly growing—part of her reveled in it. Knox was in control right now. He could do anything he wanted to her, and she'd be helpless to stop him.

No, she'd be desperate for it.

"Is that so?" He leaned in, his eyes piercing. Aria shuddered beneath him as he lowered his head to the base of her neck, lips brushing against her sensitive skin. He planted kisses there, letting his tongue trail between the small gap in her collar. Her whole body ached in response, and she arched up against him, desperately wanting to feel the press of his hard length against her. "What would you do now? When you're at my mercy?"

She moaned, writhing beneath him. She wanted to beg him to let her up. Or to beg him for more. But Aria had never known how to refuse a challenge, and it had gotten her in trouble more than once. She grinned at the glowering dragon. "I'd use my free hand."

His expression grew puzzled for a second before his eyes darkened as she reached out and stroked the hard length of his cock through his pants. He thrust into it, straining through the fabric. "Aria," he whispered, leaning even closer.

She kissed him, hungry, hot, and wet. Her

tongue found his, drawing him close to her. He groaned again as she stroked him through the fabric, teasing him to greater hardness.

He tugged her hand away, pinned it down as he pulled back from the kiss. They stayed like that for a moment, frozen there, him towering over her like she was his war prize.

Her nipples were tight little buds, and her sex was wet and aching for him.

"No," he said, his breath coming hard and fast. "We shouldn't—"

"Knox—" It came out more desperate than she meant. If she had any leverage at all, she would have kissed him, stroked him, done something to stoke the flames roaring to life between them.

But she was completely at his mercy.

Knox let go of her and stood. "I think that's enough practice for today." He left her lying there on the floor.

Aria rolled over and smushed her face into the mat, letting the surface swallow her scream of frustration.

CHAPTER EIGHT

Knox could still feel the phantom press of Aria's body against him hours later. He was a fool, an utter idiot. Nothing else could explain the madness that came from suggesting they grapple. He knew he wanted her, she wanted him. But she was keeping secrets. Everything about her might be a lie.

Yet he still wanted her to be his.

He groaned and slumped back in the chair in his office, pressing his palms to his forehead. He couldn't have her, not now. No matter that his cock twitched at the tiniest thought. It would have taken nothing to have her there, on the mat, just the two of them. She'd been just as willing as he was.

Would it really be so bad to take that step?

He pulled up the security feeds to remind

himself of his suspicions. And there she was, showing him just how much of a fool he was. Just before he'd found her in the sitting room, Aria had tried the door to his office, only to be rebuffed by one of his maids. He played the video a second time, looking for a hint of something. There was no subterfuge, no hint that she was anything other than lost.

But Knox couldn't believe it.

He'd been thinking about the bird. Aria hadn't said a word about the creature she'd rescued, and he hadn't asked. He had the strangest sense that she was embarrassed about the stunt. But he'd seen just how nimble she'd been climbing branches with a delicate being in her pocket. Not everyone could manage that, and yet she'd done it like it was nothing.

He tried his IDA contact again, but the bastard didn't answer. Knox hadn't heard a peep from him since getting confirmation of Aria's match and receiving notification of her scheduled arrival time. How busy was the man that he couldn't reply to a single comm message?

His comm buzzed with an incoming call. Soren.

Knox was tempted to ignore it. Soren would only have bad news, and Knox didn't want to hear it. Not if it was about Aria. He touched the screen to engage the call anyway. He couldn't ignore these problems.

"What is it?" His greeting wasn't pleasant.

Soren raised an eyebrow. "You're in a good mood."

Knox just scowled. "Do you have an update?"

His brother nodded, expression dire. "I'm sending through a file. I found your girl, and it wasn't easy. Greendeyl Prison Colony doesn't like to give up its records. She was there for theft. Eighteen months."

He sat back in his chair and waited for the shock to hit. It didn't. From nearly the moment she'd appeared, he'd suspected something was wrong, and now he had proof. Aria was a thief.

"I've started the deportation paperwork," Soren said after Knox didn't reply. "All I'll need is an affidavit from you. I can have my men put her in a holding cell until this is—"

"No." The objection came out before he could think it through.

"No?" Soren asked.

"She may have been a criminal in the past, but she hasn't committed a crime here. I won't see her thrown in a cell for the sins of her past."

Soren gave him a look that spoke volumes. "She's a con-artist."

"Or she's trying to turn her life around." The words felt like lies on his tongue. "Send me what paperwork I need to sign. I need time to think."

His brother disengaged the call and Knox was left wondering what in all the hells he should do. Had she lied to the IDA?

Knox pushed out of his seat and strode into the hallway and up the stairs to Aria's room. He barged in, not bothering to knock, and couldn't keep the glare from his face.

Aria startled and jumped up from the chair, the book she'd been reading falling to the floor with a thump. "Is something the matter?"

"Greendeyl—" was all he managed to say before Aria crouched in a fluid motion, scooped her fallen book up, and chucked it at his head.

Knox didn't think, he just reacted, casting a fire-ball to hover in the door to keep Aria from fleeing. They needed to *talk*.

Aria glared at him for half a second before her eyes narrowed in determination and she pointed herself straight towards the door. She covered her head with her arms and plowed straight for the fire.

Knox was frozen, unsure of how to react as she plunged into the flame.

But she didn't scream in pain. Instead, the fire seemed to bend around her, as if it refused to hurt her for even a second.

Impossible.

He couldn't give it another thought as he chased after her. His surprise had given her the upper hand, and Aria was already at the bottom of the stairs and opening the front door by the time he reached the end of the hallway.

Instead of going down, he went up.

The door to the roof banged open and he sprinted for the edge, launching himself off and shifting in midair. It only took a moment to spot Aria's form running down the street, darting around people and dodging carts. He heard one or two curses, but Aria didn't pause, not even when she had to vault over a large planter filled with delicate flowers.

She had nowhere to go, no money, and no ride off the planet.

Unless she had accomplices.

The smart move would be to let her run to her accomplices and round everyone up at once, but Knox was a being of pure instinct right now. He dived low, and even though nearly everyone on the street could turn into a dragon themselves, he still heard a scream or two. Aria darted into an alley between houses.

There was only one place for her to go.

The entrance to the park was open and Aria ran inside. Knox was already waiting and the second she passed onto the path, he breathed a massive wave of fire, circling her in and trapping her. There was too much this time for her to chance running through it.

Knox dove for the ground, shifting in the process and landing on one knee before standing up and stalking towards the only woman who'd ever made him burn.

"Why?" He grabbed her arm to hold her in place.

Aria stared up at him, but she didn't struggle. "You'll have to kill me, dragon."

He knew his fire was flaring in his eyes, he could see it reflected in the way hers widened. Knox did the only thing he could.

He kissed her.

CHAPTER NINE

UNDER ANY OTHER CIRCUMSTANCES, Aria would get lost in this kiss. Kissing Knox felt like coming home, and she wanted that. She wished she deserved it. But the fire all around them teased her nose, and the kiss turned harsh. Punishing.

She shoved him away and stumbled back, the heat of the flames licking her back. Aria didn't know how she'd avoided getting burned when she ran through the fire before, but she wasn't about to test her luck again. There was no getting away a second time.

Her luck had finally run out.

Was an angry dragon worse than Imperium justice?

She watched Knox warily as he raised his hand

to his face and ran his thumb over his lips. He watched her watch him, and his eyes seemed to swirl with the same fire that surrounded them. Did it have to be so freaking sexy?

This was why you weren't supposed to fall for the mark. Aria should have been figuring her way out of this mess, instead she couldn't stop looking at Knox and wishing things were different.

She tried to reassure herself with the fact that she hadn't actually stolen anything. Yet. In her mad dash out of the townhouse, she'd left her glasses behind, and she cursed herself for forgetting that evidence of her intent. They'd been blinking at her for hours, harmlessly reminding her that she could betray Knox at any time she wanted.

Problem was, she didn't want to.

From the way his shoulders heaved, he didn't care that his vault was safe for now.

Aria didn't say anything. His mention of Greendeyl brought up every terrible memory of her time there and she wasn't going back, not ever.

"Why are you here?" Knox asked. He kept a couple of feet between them, but there wasn't any more space for either of them to go. Strangely, his fire wasn't making it too hot in their little circle. A small, definitely insane, part of her was tempted to reach back and touch it.

"Why do you think?" Anything she said could be used against her, and there was no hope for a fair trial when the person accusing her was a damned lord.

"I know you're a thief. I know you went to prison. And I know the IDA sent you here to me. What I don't understand is why. So tell me." He managed to loom, even with the space between them.

So he hadn't realized the IDA had no idea who she was. It was why Ragnar had needed her to do the job. He'd managed to hack the IDA system and set himself up as Knox's point of contact. Aria was one of the only people he knew who fit any of the criteria Knox had been looking for.

"Why, Aria? Is that even your real name?" His anger was bleeding into disappointment, and that cut even deeper.

"It is." Part of this job meant always having the next lie ready and keeping your true self as far out of it as possible. But for the past couple of days, Aria had been nothing *but* herself. "I'm sorry." The apology got choked up in her throat, and she felt useless tears trying to form.

In a breath, the fire around them disappeared, sucked into Knox as if it had never been there. He stepped closer and hugged her. Aria collapsed into it, her arms clinging to him as she buried her face in his shirt but refused to let the tears come. His scent surrounded her, familiar already after only a few days. His arms were wrapped around her waist, and they stayed like that for a long minute.

Strangest interrogation ever.

"What happened?" he asked again, but this time, the accusation was gone. "Let me help you."

Those words had to be a lie. They had to be some sort of trick to get her to incriminate herself so he could throw her in the bottom of the deepest, darkest hole they had on this planet and forget about her.

But he wouldn't be hugging her so tightly if he wanted to forget her.

"I tried to go straight after prison," she said, the words quiet, nearly swallowed up by the fabric of his shirt. "I don't know how to do anything else, but I thought I could try. But with the stay at Greendeyl on my record, no one was willing to hire me. My accounts—the secret ones no court has ever found —were empty, and I was barely scraping by. That's when... my contact found me." She stumbled over that part. Aria didn't sell people out. It might shorten a person's sentence, but it would shorten their *life* when word got around. "I've known him since I was fourteen. I ran with his crew for a while after I was kicked out of the orphanage."

"Fourteen?" His arms tightened around her.

It was so normal in her world that she sometimes forgot how young she'd been. Aria didn't let that stop her. "He wanted me to steal a diamond from you. He got me in as your IDA match and here we are. There was no gropey captain. No stolen stuff. And I'm sorry, Knox. I didn't want to take this job in the first place, and I've wanted to do it less and less every second I'm around you. If you let me walk away, I promise you'll never see me again. I won't set foot on Vemion."

He let her go, but he didn't step back. "If you didn't want to take the job, why did you?"

"No money." She shrugged. But the lie stuck in her throat, and Aria added, "And, well, Ragnar loves to use the carrot and stick approach. He's the one who emptied my accounts—for safekeeping, he swears." Knox snorted at that, and Aria, strangely, found herself biting back a smile. It slid off her face as she said the rest of it. "And he threatened to hand me over to the Imperium for a crime that I *swear* I had nothing to do with. I never touched Imperium jobs. But their bounty hunters won't listen to reason if they find me. The price of my freedom was..."

"A diamond."

"You."

They said it at the same time, gazes locking. The connection to him felt fundamental, like walking away would tear out some part of her for good. But she had to do it. She couldn't do this job. Everything had always been fake. There was no IDA psychic calling them a perfect match, no fate that had brought them together.

The chemistry might have been boiling hot, but it couldn't matter.

"Come home with me." He held out a hand. "Let me help you get out of this mess."

"I just told you I was going to steal from you." He couldn't mean it. It had to be some kind of play. His brother, the cop, could be ready to swoop down with reinforcements at any minute. But he wouldn't need to make the offer for that to be true. They'd been standing in the open park for several minutes. Anyone could have found them by now. "That diamond is worth millions."

"I'm very aware of that." His hand didn't waver.

"You can't trust me." His hand might have been

steady, but her voice wasn't. She wanted this too much. It was every dream a thief might think of on a cold night after a job gone bad.

"And yet—" His hand was still there. "Come home with me, Aria."

She placed her hand in his.

CHAPTER TEN

Aria followed Knox back to the townhouse in a sort of daze. This wasn't how she saw this job going. She was supposed to get in, get out, and get the diamond. Then she would be sucked back into Ragnar's circle and forced into the career she'd been trying to leave behind.

Just because she didn't want that future, didn't mean she couldn't see it unfolding before her.

Now that future was a mystery. Since when did she tell her victims about a job? But Knox wasn't any mark. He was special.

And she believed him when he said he could get her out of this mess. She hoped with all her heart that he was right.

The walk back was subdued, and Aria felt a hint

of guilt when she saw someone on the street trying to right an overturned cart that she had played a part in tipping over on her run from Knox. She kept her eyes forward the rest of the way back.

"Would you like to see it?" he asked once they were safely in his house.

"See what?" She'd had free run of the public parts of his house for the past couple of days and had taken an inventory of all of the baubles and treasures he had on display. It was quite the collection. And she would be lying if she said that her itchy fingers hadn't wanted to snatch a few things on principle. That wasn't about stealing from the guy, that was just... training.

"The diamond," he said, as if it were obvious.

"I tell you that I'm coming to steal a massive diamond, maybe the biggest one in the universe, and you're just going to take me down to the vault and show it to me?" She couldn't keep the disbelief out of her voice.

"So you know it's in the vault," he said, and nodded in confirmation. "You came all this way. And I'm going to put it on display anyway. I want people to see my collection, to enjoy it. What's the use if it's just locked up in a vault forever?"

"Then why is it there now?" she asked.

"I'm not going to display until I have the proper security in place. We wouldn't want thieves getting there." The look her way was pointed, but his eyes were bright.

Despite herself, a small smile tugged at Aria's lips. "Yeah, I'd like to see it." How could she resist?

She expected that he would take her to a discreet staircase somewhere, something that looked like it was just for the servants. She knew the vault was below the house. Instead he took her to a small elevator whose door only opened after Knox scanned his palm print and his eye. Then he summoned a flick of fire and held it under what looked like a heat sensor.

"What are you doing?" Professional curiosity had her wondering about the security system. And, she realized that if these were the measures to get down to the vault, opening the door from the inside was the least of her troubles.

"There's a sensor on the bottom that scans my hand for some markers that indicate it's me. The sensor on the top analyzes the properties of dragon fire. It's not as simple as lighting a match and holding it above your hand." The elevator door opened and they stepped in.

They descended for several seconds before the

door slid open to reveal a short hallway with a massive vault door at the end of it.

"Here it is," he said. "My cave of treasures."

"Your hoard?" she suggested.

Knox gave her an assessing look, one Aria couldn't quite decipher. "Something like that."

The vault was secure, she was sure. But there were no biometric features. He entered a code on the keypad and then spun the wheel lock until the door clicked open.

Excitement simmered in her veins. Aria had seen the inside of more than one vault in her life, but this was different. Knox's invitation meant that she could savor this moment, that she didn't need to be in and out in under a minute. She could see everything he had and ask questions, to indulge her curiosity about goods rather than just nick whatever she was after.

Lights automatically turned on as they stepped inside, and the door shut behind them.

"Don't worry about that," Knox reassured her. "We can open it from in here. It's perfectly safe."

"I do know a thing or two about vaults," Aria reminded him.

He nodded, but didn't seem put off by it. "How were you going to do it? I know exactly how good the door on this vault is. I put a lot of money into my security systems. The door wouldn't just open for you."

It was one thing to accept his help, and another completely to reveal her secrets. But Aria knew she had to do it. If she started withholding now, there was no way Knox would continue to help her. And, now that she was on his side, maybe she didn't want someone else waltzing in and stealing from him.

If she didn't get to take his stuff, no one did.

She held up a finger and crouched down, looking along the edge of the vault wall for her small robot. And there it was, little more than a thick speck of dust that seemed to shrink into itself as she approached. She plucked it up and ran her finger over it until the device expanded and it was nearly the size of her palm.

"Meet my little friend." She showed it to Knox, noting that the light on top was blinking. It was still transmitting the signal to her glasses, the ones that were upstairs and would have given everything away if Knox had bothered to search her room. "This device mapped your house. And if I were to give it a signal from my glasses, it would engage the failsafe and open the door from the inside. No safecracking needed."

"I knew there was something up with those glasses," said Knox. He held out a hand. "May I see it?"

Aria pressed the button to turn off the transmission just in case someone else was listening in and handed it over to him. "I think they were originally created to map rubble after landslides or something. We figured out the other uses. They're expensive as sin though."

"I thought you said you didn't have any money."

"The guy who hired me for the job gave me my tools," she said. "I couldn't have afforded this myself."

Knox studied the robot for a moment before slipping it into his pocket and then nodding towards the back corner of the vault.

Aria kind of expected a pedestal with a spotlight and other elements of display. Instead there was a small black box with a handprint lock and a keypad on top of it. Knox unlocked it and removed the lid.

"Stars above!" The words escaped her mouth without thought, and Aria stepped closer, brushing up against Knox's side. "Can I touch it?" It was bigger than her fist, completely impractical and ostentatious, and so clear that she could practically see through it. Diamonds weren't her favorite gem. She'd always thought they were a bit boring. But this one was the size of a ball and so ridiculous that she couldn't help but want to get close to it.

Knox handed it over, and the weight was surprisingly heavy. She studied it for a moment, tempted to place it in her pocket and run. Not to hand it over to Ragnar. Just to teach Knox a lesson about handing gems to thieves.

Ex-thieves. Maybe.

She would have to figure that out. She handed it back to him before the temptation became too great.

If there was anything strange in the way Aria was acting, Knox didn't comment. "I need some time to do a little research," he said. "Meet me in my office in the morning?"

It wasn't like she had another choice.

And when Aria slept that night, she dreamt of Knox, chasing her, holding her, fucking her. Burning her to ash.

The whispers and shadows of the dream washed away in the morning and she found herself surprisingly rested. She met him in his office after breakfast and plopped down into the guest chair.

"Ready to send me away?" she couldn't stop herself from asking. She should be grateful, she knew, but Aria didn't know how to take a gift. Everything she'd ever had, it felt like she stole.

Knox looked more serious than usual. "I know you said that you didn't sign up for the Intergalactic Dating Agency. You aren't here to find a husband."

"I think we've established pretty well why I came here." What was he thinking?

He let that slide and spoke. "The nobility of this planet are exempt from extradition. Even to the Imperium."

"That sounds nice for you," said Aria. Nobility always found a way to stay clear of trouble.

"It could be nice for you too." He slid a piece of paper across the desk towards her.

Application for Marriage. That was what the top line read. "What's that supposed to be?"

Knox spoke as if he weren't trying to fundamentally alter the state of... everything. "If we were to marry, you would be safe. No one could take you off this planet. Not unless you left of your own volition."

Aria was already shaking her head. "You can't want to marry me. All you know about me is that I'm a thief. That I came here to rob you. What are you thinking?" Did his brother know he was thinking about this? Maybe she should tell him. Maybe *somebody* needed to get his head checked.

"Ex-thief," was all Knox said.

"We can't just get married. There has to be another way." A small part of her wanted to jump for joy. Wanted to kiss the man and say that of course she'd be his, even if it was just to keep her out of prison or to escape execution. She'd done far worse things with far less prompting.

But saying yes felt like just another level of taking advantage of Knox. "You can't want me like that."

His eyes flicked up and down, a flicker of flame flaring in his gaze for a moment. "We both felt this thing between us. Whether the IDA was involved or not, there's something there. The marriage doesn't need to be forever. It buys us time. We'll find a way to more permanently clear your name."

That should have made Aria feel better. It was just another con. Another short-term solution to get her what she wanted. "I need to think about this." She stood. "This isn't a no. I'm not running away. I just need to go think. I'll be back later." She left the office before he could say anything else.

When she was outside and on the streets, she turned away from the park. It held too many memories of yesterday. Too many memories of Knox. She walked a few blocks towards the main part of the city and looked in the windows of the bakeries and dressmakers, pausing in front of the hat shop and taking in the display.

Could this place be her home? Could she really say yes to Knox, even if it was only for a little while? Was she really ready to marry a dragon lord?

Would that make her a lady?

If only the people from the orphanage could see her now. And what would Ragnar think about it? He sent her off to rob a guy and she ended up marrying him. He would be *so* pissed off.

That made her smile for a moment. The smile slipped off her face as she kept walking. She ended up in a small courtyard in the middle of the city and sat on a bench. Ragnar wouldn't let this go. He'd come for her. And he might hurt Knox in the process.

Yes, she knew Knox was a dragon.

He could handle himself in a fight. She'd seen those muscles. Felt them up close.

But Ragnar didn't fight fair. And he'd ensure that Knox paid for her crimes.

She had to tell Knox no. If only to protect him. So why did it hurt so much to think of the denial?

Aria stood and started heading back towards the townhouse. There had to be another way.

She'd only taken two steps when a person in full Imperium bounty hunter armor, their face covered by a black helmet and mask, teleported in front of her, blaster already pointed her way.

Instinct had Aria diving to the side to avoid the shot. She took off running for cover.

Why were they here? How had they found out?

She was going to hunt Ragnar down and murder him.

The people on the street were already screaming, and she could hear and feel the impact of the blaster shots as they singed the brick building around her.

Aria kept sprinting. Yeah, she couldn't outrun a flying dragon, but the bounty hunter was on two feet. He was still just a person.

But Imperium hunters didn't stop. They didn't give up on finding their prey. They were almost supernatural in their dogged pursuit.

She had to get back to Knox. Knox would keep her safe.

At the end of the alley, she froze. All that was left in front of her was an open park that sprawled across a city block. The trees were barely more than twigs. There was no cover. If she ran for it, the hunter would shoot her like it was nothing. If she stayed still, he would catch her in less than a minute.

She had to take her chances.

Aria sprinted and zagged to the side just before a shot could hit her straight in the back.

Get down! The words echoed in her head and Aria dove for the ground as dragon fire exploded behind her, stopping the hunter in his tracks.

Knox landed in his dragon form and his voice echoed in her head again. *Get on*, he commanded.

She didn't know how he was talking to her. Were dragons somehow telepathic?

No time for questions.

She climbed on his back and he burst up into the air, climbing so fast she had trouble sucking in a breath.

Aria clutched at his scales and prayed she didn't fall off.

CHAPTER ELEVEN

THE AIR WHIPPED her hair around her head, and all of Aria's muscles were clenched, as if that might do something to keep her connected to the dragon she was riding.

She was *riding* a dragon.

What. The. Hell.

And what the hell were those Imperium bounty hunters doing on Vemion?

There wasn't any time to wonder as Knox banked and she found herself leaning into it. This ride would have almost been fun, if it weren't for the threat of imprisonment and death that had led up to it.

She had a good idea of the layout of the city, but Knox didn't go back to his townhouse. That flight would have only taken a minute and the bounty hunter would have caught up in no time. So where was he taking her?

The dragon she knew was definitely better than the bounty hunter she didn't, but part of Aria was still braced for betrayal. After all, she'd walked out on Knox's proposal. She'd come to him trying to steal his stuff. Why wouldn't he betray her? Did it even count as betrayal when she was the one who came under false pretenses?

She shivered against the wind and after a while lost track of time. They'd been flying forever, possibly. One thing was certain, the bounty hunter wouldn't catch up anytime soon.

Knox didn't try and talk to her telepathically anymore, and Aria didn't think anything his way. She was worried that if she started, all of her thoughts might start leaking out, and he didn't need to know exactly how he'd been appearing in her dreams.

Oh gods, could he hear her thoughts now?

If he could, he gave no indication.

They passed a long line of shallow hills and Knox began to descend. Once they were a bit lower, Aria spotted a road weaving through the hills and farther into the countryside. There were narrower roads, maybe driveways, that branched off the main path, but she didn't see houses.

Was that a warehouse?

Whatever it was, it was where Knox landed. The building wasn't much to look at, a squat square with tall, narrow windows all around it and a large garage that suggested it might be used for storage or shipping.

But she didn't see any vehicles outside or any other signs of commerce. And though they'd been flying high, she would have seen cities or towns nearby, and there were none. Whatever this place was meant to be, it wasn't here because it was convenient.

Knox shifted back to his human form, and his gaze, when he met hers, was serious. Aria had the strangest urge to apologize, which wouldn't get either of them anywhere.

He held out his hand and she took it, feeling a little more at ease as their fingers intertwined. How odd. She'd never let anyone get close before, never felt the pitter patter of her heartbeat when someone took her hand or tucked her hair behind her ear. But three days with Knox, a person she wasn't supposed to feel *anything* for, and she was questioning everything.

Knox led her around the building to a regular door. The inside only invited more questions. Definitely not a warehouse. The floor was carpeted and the walls were painted in bright colors, with crude, almost childish designs at hip level and below. Were there kids here? She didn't hear anything, but the walls could be thick.

"We'll be safe here," Knox promised. "At least for now. Nothing connects me to this place."

"What *is* this place?" she asked. They walked down the narrow hallway and up three flights of stairs to the top floor. The hallway on that floor terminated in a large locked door, but Knox opened a smaller door that led to a small bedroom. There was a bed flanked by two night tables, two of those thin windows she'd spotted from outside, and another door that might have led to a bathroom.

Huh.

"I have more money than sense, some have said." Knox flicked on the light and closed the door behind her. "This is the place where I try to do some good with it."

"What kind of good?" None of the research Ragnar had given her had indicated that Knox was anything more than a treasure hunter who liked to revel in his riches.

"We can talk about that later. Are you hurt?" He crossed the room to her and placed a gentle hand on her shoulder.

"I'm fine." Shaken, still wondering about how she'd been found, and desperate not to bring more trouble down on this man, but uninjured. "How —" She cut herself off. Any more words in that question might sound like an accusation. Instead, she placed her hand over Knox's and leaned into his touch, wrapping her free hand around his waist.

They stood like that for a long moment, the heat wafting off of him a comfort that grounded her in a way that nothing ever had before. She could come to need this man, she knew. It wouldn't take much. He was so solid, so *there*, and he wanted to help.

Though she'd been determined to turn him down, more and more of her wanted to say yes.

She looked up and met the eyes of the dragon who'd come to save her. He opened his mouth, but Aria was done talking. She surged up and kissed him.

His response was immediate, strong hands gripping her tighter, one hand coming up to tangle in her hair, and lips parting to draw her in. She whimpered into the kiss, relief and desire and the release of pent up energy roaring into an inferno so hot she was amazed they didn't go up in flames.

Knox nipped at her lips before sweeping his tongue into her mouth. Aria moaned into the caress and brought her hands around his neck to hold him closer. He groaned and hoisted her up until she wrapped her legs around his waist.

Aria couldn't get enough of him, wanted to explore every inch of his body, to learn and memorize his taste and how he smelled and everything she could about this dragon man.

Their clothing seemed to dissolve away under their hands. Knox tossed her on the bed and pulled off her boots and pants, leaving her in a pair of plain gray panties. She blushed when he knelt between her knees, but Knox just grinned at her, and lowered his head, kissing his way up her thigh as if she was the most precious thing in the world.

As he hooked a finger under the fabric and tugged her underwear off, Aria couldn't look away. Her skin pebbled into goosebumps, and she could feel the wetness growing between her thighs. Knox smiled and ran a single finger over the slick folds, and Aria gasped with pleasure. She rocked against his hand, desperate for more.

Then he stopped. He moved up her body until

his lips hovered over hers. "I don't care how you got here," he told her, the intensity in his gaze undeniable. "I don't care what you've done in the past. I don't care if the whole Imperium is coming after you. You are what I want." His kiss was fierce as he nudged her lips open and thrust his tongue inside.

Aria couldn't contain her moan and arched against him. He held her firmly and kissed her until she was trembling with need. When he finally pulled back, they were both breathing hard, and he looked so gorgeous, wild, and untamed that she couldn't believe she was lucky enough to be here with him.

Knox trailed his lips down her neck and then further, pausing when he reached her breasts. He teased her there, laving and suckling and using his fingers to pluck at her nipples until she was mindless with need. Then he moved on, kissing his way down her abdomen.

By the time he got to her core, Aria was sure she would combust. Then his lips closed over her sensitive nub and she couldn't think at all. He stroked her expertly, swirling his tongue, and alternating between soft touches and firm ones, his rhythm changing until she thought she would scream with need.

When he pushed a finger inside, her hips bucked and she threw her head back and forth, the pleasure overwhelming her, but she couldn't find the release she desperately needed. She buried her fingers in his hair and dug her heel into his back, pleading with him for more.

A second finger joined the first, and Knox increased the tempo of his attention until Aria screamed as she climaxed, clamping down on him as a rush of sensation shot through her and the world faded to white.

She might have blacked out for a few seconds, and when she came to, Aria blinked up at the ceiling and then gasped when she saw Knox poised above her, hard cock in his hand. His fingers brushed against her core and she felt herself clench in response. "Are you ready?" he asked her, and Aria nodded, still too tongue tied for speech. This connection with Knox was like finding a part of herself that had been missing, but she didn't have the words to say it.

Knox positioned himself between her thighs and slowly slid inside. He was big, and he filled her so fully Aria gasped. But the pressure was exquisite, and she rocked her hips to take him deeper. Knox growled and slammed the rest of the way home. He captured her cry with a kiss and pinned her arms above her head as he thrust in and out, taking her higher with every stroke.

Her dragon moved faster, the friction nearly perfect as he fucked her hard and fast, and when he dropped his head to lick and then nibble her breast, Aria moaned, her body quivering with pleasure as she approached the peak once again. She felt Knox tense and then stiffen, his teeth scraping gently over her nipple as he came and she was swept along with him.

She clutched at him, the cries ripped from her throat as her body shattered with pleasure, until they were both limp and exhausted. Knox rolled onto his side, and arranged Aria so she was tucked next to him, safe and protected in his embrace.

"Rest," he said. "We'll be safe for tonight."

And the craziest part of the already crazy day was that she believed him.

CHAPTER TWELVE

The orphanage was the safest place Knox could think to go on short notice. On paper, it had little connection to him. Sure, he was one of the donors who sent plenty of funds there on an annual basis, but no one knew that he had a much closer hand in running the place.

He couldn't just sit on a pile of jewels all day and admire their shininess. He needed to do something. And helping the orphaned children of his planet was fulfilling in a way he hadn't expected when it all began.

The children were running circles around Aria, who kept spinning around, trying to keep sight of them. Every so often, she would throw her head back and laugh so openly that it made his heart ache.

It was becoming more and more obvious to him that she was his mate. She had listened when he spoke into her mind, something he should have only been able to do with another dragon. He was almost certain she had controlled his flame on more than one occasion. Only his mate could do that.

And it certainly felt like fate had put her in his path.

Aria had to physically pull herself away from two of the younger children before she came up to him and threw herself down into the chair on the side of the recreation room. "They're happy," she said, sounding a bit surprised.

"They're children. Why shouldn't they be happy?"

Her face grew pensive. "I would say I grew up in a place like this, but it was really nothing like this. We had a few dolls and old cars and trucks to play with, but they were all more than thirty years old and broken. And there weren't nearly enough for all of us. It was always so cold in winter. We had to fit as many kids into one bed as we could just to share warmth. Our blankets were tissue thin. I'm not sure I ever laughed there."

He had seen the expression on her face when he told her what this place was after they woke up. He'd suspected her childhood was nothing like the charmed existence he had led. But hearing it in her voice made him want to hunt down whoever had mistreated her as a child and make them pay. He couldn't do that. But he could make sure that every day going forward she had exactly what she needed.

That she had him.

She hadn't responded to his proposal, and Knox had enough self-preservation to keep from asking again. If she was eager to say yes, she would have done it already. So he would have to find a way to convince her, and not for anything as flimsy as keeping the Imperium away from her.

She was his mate. He was keeping her for good.

He reached out and grabbed her hand, lacing their fingers together. "My parents were big on volunteering when I was a kid, and if we didn't choose something, then they chose for us. I was definitely a little shit."

She smiled and said nothing, but her eyes said everything. "Of course you were."

Knox lifted her hand up and kissed it. "I started volunteering at another orphanage with kids who were closer to my age. Maybe it scared the shit out of me the first time I showed up; it did *not* go well." That startled a laugh out of her, and Knox continued. "But I came back, and eventually I got older and came in to part of my inheritance, and I realized that I wanted to help. So I set up this place. It's a home for these kids, a school, and it gives them a place to heal—all of them lost parents in sudden and tragic ways. They need that space. The city is too loud, too close."

"Nothing in your file says you help orphans," she commented.

"Surely there's a note about philanthropy."

"Philanthropy, yes... but nothing like this."

One of the little girls, no more than seven years old, let out a howl of laughter and sprinted up to Aria, grabbing her free hand. "Come on," she demanded. "We need you to judge our race."

Aria looked at him. "Duty calls."

He kissed her hand once more and let go. "I need to call my brother. I have some questions about yesterday."

She nodded, her face serious for a moment before she turned back to the child, her expression bright and smiling.

Knox would have rather sat there all day and watched them play. Aria deserved the carefree freedom that came from playing with these children. She deserved to lay down her burdens.

He was going to find a way to make that possible.

He went to the room where they'd stayed the night. Normally, it was a bedroom for one of the guardians who oversaw the children on the third floor, but that position was currently empty.

He pulled out his communicator and gave Soren a call. His brother answered quickly. "You caused quite a stir," he said.

"An Imperium bounty hunter. What did you *do*?" Soren was the only other person who knew that Aria wasn't everything she seemed, and Knox hadn't told him half of it.

"I haven't done anything," he said, enunciating each word. "I wouldn't call in the Imperium. Our uncle would never allow the violation of our sovereignty."

"Uncle" was not quite the correct term for the king, but it worked well enough. And that was true. If Soren was anything, he was loyal. "If you didn't call them in, who did?" The Imperium didn't stop once they got a scent, not unless they were given a different target.

"Would it be so bad to let them take her?" Soren

asked. He held up a hand when Knox made an outraged sound. "She's a thief, you know that. She's not a citizen of this planet. Perhaps it would just be easier for interplanetary relations if this problem just went away."

"She's my mate!" Knox slammed his hand down on a table. "They can't have her."

His brother looked mildly surprised, but only mildly. Knox had been adamant about Aria from the first, he knew. His brother, no doubt, thought something was up.

"Congratulations," Soren said with a slight hint of sarcasm. "That does make this more complicated."

"Do I look like I care? How do we get rid of the problem?"

"I have the city guard looking for the bounty hunter. I doubt we'll find that person. Imperium hunters are not exactly known for getting caught. Keep your mate out of sight for a bit longer. This may take some wrangling."

Knox agreed and said goodbye to his brother before ending the call. He had to keep Aria safe. He just wished he knew how.

———

Aria judged at least a dozen races among the class of seven-year-olds that she had been observing all morning. There were eight of them, all orphans, all with huge eyes and bright smiles. They didn't look like kids who had been dealt a hard blow by the world, even if tragedy had rocked their young lives. They knew they were safe. They had space to heal.

Knox was providing that for them.

The kids plopped down in a circle on the floor, and one of them dragged her right along with them. Maybe they could sense that she had once been one of them. She didn't know what had made her an orphan. Had she been abandoned? Kidnapped? Had her parents died? If it was noted in a file somewhere, that information had been lost a long time ago. Aria had taught herself not to care. But sitting in this room, among these kids, was bringing up some memories that would be better left dormant.

"Are you Lord Knox's wife?" one of the kids, she thought his name was Rex, asked. The kid beside him gave him a scandalized look but then looked toward her, his expression eager.

Aria laughed nervously. "No, I'm not married." And she was trying hard not to think of Knox's proposal. If she didn't feel good enough to marry him when he was just some super rich guy who was kind of nice, how was she good enough to marry him when he was a super rich guy who spent all his money on keeping orphans happy?

The night before was amazing. It was everything she could have wished for, and a small part of her had almost cried from the joy of it. Thankfully, she hadn't, because then she would've had to flee in the night just to keep her reputation safe. She didn't cry in front of other people.

She wanted him again. But that wasn't anything new. She had wanted him from the start. And she definitely wasn't going to talk about that in front of the children.

"You're not a dragon," said another one of the kids.

"No, I'm not," she agreed. "I'm human. Do you guys know what humans are?" As far as she could tell, all of these orphans were baby dragons. She had seen a bit of steaming smoke, but no fire, and no one had shifted. There were probably rules for that kind of thing.

The kids nodded. At least she didn't have to explain.

"Lord Knox has never brought a girl here before."

"Not," said another kid. "He brought that lady. She brought the fruit basket."

"And the chocolates!" added another kid.

"Those were supposed to be a secret," the first kid reminded his friends.

"Wasn't that Lord Knox's sister?" the quietest of the kids said, a little girl sitting in the back, her blonde hair in twin braids on either side of her head.

The kids conversed among themselves for a moment. Aria was in no rush to hurry them up.

"Are you his mate?" the girl with the braids asked.

"Mate?" Aria had heard of such things, of course. A person didn't travel across star systems without learning about the different ways that certain societies handled their romantic relationships. Mate could mean anything. In some places, it meant friend; in others, lover. And in some places, it was a fated companion or perhaps some sort of biological connection. Something special.

What she felt for Knox sure felt special.

"I'm not sure what that means," she told the girl.

The kid clambered forward, eyes wide and mouth set in frustration. "My mom and dad were mates."

"Oh. That's a good thing," Aria hoped. She wasn't exactly sure how she was supposed to approach that situation. She didn't want any of the kids to start crying in grief over lost loved ones.

One of the kids chimed in with more. "It's when you can control someone else's fire. Not just your own."

"I don't have fire," Aria reminded them all gently. Perhaps seven-year-old dragonlings did not have the best grasp on what exactly a human was. But she remembered running out of her bedroom at Knox's townhouse. Was that only yesterday? Was that only two days ago? She'd flung her hands up in front of her and waved his fire away. It had moved.

"And somebody's fire doesn't hurt you. But we can't test that," one of the little boys said. "Because we could really hurt someone."

"What about speaking to my mind? When he's in his dragon form?" she asked.

"We can all talk to each other like that! But only when we're all in dragon form," one kid said. "Can't you speak mind to mind?"

"Interesting." Aria was tempted to ask more of the children, but seven-year-olds weren't exactly known for their accuracy, and she feared she might get some very distorted ideas if she kept on this path.

"Did bad people try to hurt you?" Rex asked. He

leaned against her, resting his head against her arm. "Bad people got my mom and dad. That's why I had to come here. Is that why you had to come here?"

"Lord Knox just wanted to show me this special place," she lied. "He told me that the fastest runners in the entire planet are here. I think we've rested enough. Who wants to race one more time? I need to know who's the fastest."

The kids sprung up and sprinted for the starting line.

Aria kept a pleasant expression pasted on her face. But Rex's innocent question had her reeling. This place might not be connected on paper to Knox, but eventually the bounty hunter would find her. And she couldn't let any risk come to these kids.

This was her mess. She wasn't going to let anyone else get hurt.

CHAPTER THIRTEEN

Aria looked out the window at the starry night sky. Every extra moment she stayed at the orphanage put all those kids at risk. But where else was she supposed to go? Ragnar was still out there. Even worse, so was the Imperium. They didn't know she was here. Not yet. It couldn't last. Nothing ever did.

If she had a bag, it would've already been packed. But all she had were the clothes she came in. That should have made it easier. All she had to do was flee, to disappear into the darkness, never to be seen again.

Easier said than done.

She and Knox were in the middle of nowhere. They would see anyone coming for them. That also meant that Knox would see anyone leaving. And she couldn't leave without saying goodbye.

Aria huffed out a hollow laugh. Her entire life, she had lived by not making connections, by not getting close, by being willing to flee at the first sign of trouble. And even that had kept her safe. But look at her now, completely entangled with the mark and hiding out among a gaggle of orphans he cared for.

She heard the door open, and she could practically feel the air move as Knox crossed the room toward her. He placed a hand on her back and rubbed up and down gently. She found herself leaning into him, chasing the sensation in a way that might have embarrassed her at any other time. But not here. Not with him.

"What's wrong?" Knox asked. "Aside from the obvious."

She leaned back more fully against him. "I can't stay here." She should have told him that hours ago. They could have already been back in the city by now. But this place was peaceful. And if this was the last peace she had in her life, she wanted to cherish it, just for a little while.

That probably made her the most selfish person on the planet, and for some reason, she actually cared about that. "Ragnar won't stop coming for me.

I failed this job. He'll send someone else. He's going to make me pay. Somehow."

Knox's hand glided from her back to around her waist, and he hugged her loosely. "He can't have you."

She wished that were true. She wished she believed that Knox's influence as a dragon lord would be enough for safety. But even if he could keep her safe in the moment, that wasn't enough for life. She couldn't just hide away on this little planet forever. Could she?

"What's the story with the two of you?"

If Aria was going to re-examine her past, she couldn't be touching Knox. She stepped away and took a seat at the small desk. Knox leaned against the wall and looked at her. "I was pretty fresh out of the orphanage when Ragnar found me. Maybe fourteen? I'm not exactly sure how old I am."

"You were kicked out of the orphanage so young?" A puff of smoke appeared around him and disappeared nearly as quickly. "Or did you run away?" Of course, that would rouse his emotions. If she were talking about someone else, Aria would have been very angry on their behalf.

But it was her story, and she was used to it. She shrugged. "Too many kids. Not enough beds. It wasn't necessarily by age that they kicked us out. It was those of us who caused trouble. Or those of us who seemed like we could make it on our own. Those that the headmistress didn't like. And it was a mix of all three with me. It could've been worse. Ragnar wanted me to steal stuff. I had sticky fingers. And for a while, it was good. I was decent at the job. He kept me clothed and fed. I was able to build up a pretty decent nest egg. But within a few years, I felt like I outgrew his crew. I wanted to take bigger jobs. And I didn't want to target people who couldn't afford to lose, you know?"

"You only wanted to steal from spoiled aristocrats with more money than sense?" Knox asked with a small smile.

Aria returned the grin. "You get me. Ragnar let me go. We stayed in touch. Occasionally I would help him out. Occasionally he would help me out. I thought it was okay. Until I got sent to the prison colony. I'm still not sure who sold me out. But it might've been him. If he needed a favor from somebody else, I know he would've given me up. He stole my money. And I told you the rest. He blackmailed me to be here. If you're nice to him, if you do what he says, he's not the worst guy out there. But he's not loyal. And when you betray him, he makes you pay. I've seen what he did to other people. I know what he threatened to do to me. And he will do it. In our world, you have to follow through on those threats."

"It doesn't have to be your world anymore," Knox reminded her. He strode across the room and offered a hand.

Aria took it, letting him pull her up out of the chair, letting him wrap his arms around her, and surrendering to his embrace.

He held her close. "He can't have you. I will do everything in my power and beyond that to make sure that you're safe."

She could feel tears pricking at the corners of her eyes, and she squeezed them shut, unwilling to let them fall. "Marry me, Aria," Knox offered again. And this time it didn't feel like a ploy meant to keep her safe from extradition.

"Am I your mate?" The children had told her enough. She could draw her own conclusions. But Knox was the one who could truly answer it.

"Yes." He whispered it right into her ear, and Aria shivered.

Then she made herself step away. She met Knox's eyes. "No. I can't marry you. I can't bring you down with me."

His eyes flashed with fire, his gaze fierce, his expression determined. "You wouldn't be bringing me down. I want to help you. Whatever it takes. And I want you free. I want you to be able to choose. To choose me... or not," he added after a moment.

That had her stepping right back up to him and clutching his hand. "You think I wouldn't choose you if I had the choice? Knox, I—I haven't gotten to want things for myself in a long time. But I want you. I want this. But I can't risk this. The Imperium doesn't give up. And Ragnar has no doubt given them enough dirt on me, some of it very possibly true, to have me thrown away without a key. They'll execute me. Eventually. He's the reason they know I'm here, I'm sure. Maybe he was tapping into the signal in the vault, maybe he just knew I couldn't go through with this. He's going to make me pay."

"He won't." Knox was adamant. "You've taken risks before," he said. "Will you take one now? Will you trust me?"

There was only one answer she could give.

"Yes."

CHAPTER FOURTEEN

Aria's heart wasn't pounding. She could keep her wits together on any job, no matter how hot things got. But this was hotter than she liked.

She had the freaking diamond in a case hand-cuffed to her wrist. It was a bit over the top. But there was no way she was risking losing this thing. Not after it had nearly cost her so much. Not after it had gained her everything.

She tried not to think about ways this could go wrong. She wasn't on Vemion anymore. Whatever protection Knox could provide her, he had no power here.

But she had to make this stop. She had to do this now, to defang Ragnar and save herself and anyone else he might hurt.

It sure sounded good in her head, all noble and shit. But Aria wasn't noble, not even if she had given her heart to one of them. She was a scrappy little thing who would stab a person for table scraps. That was the life she had grown up in. That was the life she knew.

And she was going to use every single one of those skills to finish this.

The transport station was busy. This place acted as a hub in this corner of the galaxy with people passing into and out of the Imperium, though they were safely outside of Imperium territory, and for people going further afield.

It was anonymous. The kind of perfect place she had made switches and drops before. It didn't matter that the place was littered with cameras. A little bit of hair dye, a little bit of digital wizardry, a little bit of smarts, and it didn't matter.

Even if the cameras did catch her, she would normally be gone long before they had anything to do about it.

Ragnar was sitting in the food court area, his table toward the edge of the room and right near an emergency exit. They were in the heart of the space station; the exit didn't lead outside, but it would get him away from this area and on a path to the emergency escape vessels in a matter of minutes.

Aria hoped Knox would come through.

She hadn't seen him in more than a day. She didn't even have most of the details. But this was the way to get Ragnar out into the open.

The asshole thief smiled when he saw her. "I didn't think you would make it."

Aria took a seat and placed the briefcase on the table, not bothering to unhook it from her arm. "Since when do I leave a job unfinished?" she asked. The diamond really was in the case. It was going to be necessary for everything to work out right. And it occurred to her that she could just take off. She could run right now and buy a planet or three with the proceeds of ditching the rock.

Knox wouldn't come for her. At least not in a way that meant pressing charges.

But taking the stone and running meant never seeing her mate again. And that was unacceptable. No riches were worth more than him.

"What are you smiling about?" Ragnar demanded. "Let me see it."

If Ragnar hadn't made her take this job, she never would've met Knox. There was no way she would have ever ended up on the same planet as him. And she never would have signed up for something as inane as the Intergalactic Dating Agency.

"You've done a lot for me," she told Ragnar. It was sort of true. For every betrayal, there was an equal opportunity.

"There are more jobs, if you want them," Ragnar said. "I've got a little thing going down next week. I could use your skills."

"I told you I was done after this. I meant it." There wasn't even a lick of temptation. And it had very little to do with Ragnar. "My accounts?" A chair scraped somewhere in the cafeteria, and Aria had to suppress her flinch.

This could all go wrong so fast.

Ragnar pulled out a data pad and pressed a few buttons. Then he smiled at her. "All done. The money is waiting in your account. And there's even a little extra, as a thank you." He gestured at the briefcase. "Hand it over."

Instead, Aria stood. "No, I don't think I will." She pushed in her chair and turned around. "We're done, Ragnar. This is it. Just walk away." Would she let him go if he did? Irrelevant. The man didn't know how to walk away.

Aria made it three steps before Ragnar vaulted over the table and tackled her to the ground. People around them shrieked, and Aria had to suppress her instincts to fight back. It would only take one good strike to the groin for her to be able to wriggle out of Ragnar's control.

Instead, she clamped her hands down on the briefcase and kept a tight grip on it. He couldn't get that. He still tried. He tugged with all his might, the chain of the handcuff pulling enough to bruise her skin. Aria made a pained noise and tried to get away.

In the mad scuffle, the case popped open, revealing the audaciously huge diamond sitting right there on a bed of black velvet. Ragnar glared at her for a second, and he hesitated, but the diamond was right there, and he was too greedy to resist it. He snatched the gem and gave her a swift kick in the ribs before taking off sprinting toward the emergency exit.

Aria tried to get up, but something poked at her stomach, and she let out a true gasp of pain as she realized the bastard might have actually broken something. More carefully this time, she managed to sit, and she watched as an Imperium bounty hunter appeared out of nowhere and burst through the door only a second behind Ragnar.

She could hear the scuffle, and another minute later, the hunter dragged a disgruntled looking

Ragnar out of the door. Ragnar's hands were bound behind him, and the bounty hunter's belt bulged with the diamond in a special compartment.

Aria stayed down. She didn't want Ragnar seeing her. She certainly didn't want the bounty hunter to see her. This was all part of Knox's grand plan. But they couldn't guarantee that she wouldn't be caught in the crossfire.

She managed to slink away in the commotion. She found Knox waiting exactly where he was supposed to be, right at the small ship he had rented that was docked in the first-class docking area.

He took one look at her and rushed her to the med bay of the ship. The med bot took care of the rib in no time, but Knox insisted on leaving her to heal for another hour. He didn't leave her side. Not even when he received a call that made his face grow serious.

"Understood," he said and hung up.

"What is it?" she asked.

"Ragnar is in Imperium custody. He will be tried for stealing the diamond and assaulting a stranger. The assault probably won't stick when they can't find you to give testimony. But the diamond is known to be mine. Good call on the food court."

"It's owned by an Imperium company. They

consider it under their jurisdiction." She had worried Ragnar would figure that out, but the man wanted his stone and was too shortsighted to do that bit of research. "He's never going to be free again," she said. It felt a little bad, selling someone out. She'd never done it before. She had no intention of doing it again. But Ragnar had threatened everything. She wouldn't go down for him. Not when she finally had happiness in her grasp.

Knox wrapped his arms around her and pulled her close. "Let's go home."

CHAPTER FIFTEEN

One week later

Aria wrapped herself in a thick blanket and sank back into the mattress, letting the stress of her day wash away. Stress. Ha! As if she'd dealt with anything more stressful than saying how she liked her coffee since Knox brought her home.

And it *was* home now. There wasn't a single doubt in her head about that. A man didn't call a girl his mate and risk losing a diamond the size of a grapefruit for a short-lived fling. At least, Knox didn't.

The rest of the family would take a bit longer to warm up to her. When she and Knox had arrived back, the day saved and Ragnar taken care of, Soren had given her the kind of look that told her he'd be on the lookout for any trouble.

Let him look. Aria was officially retired from funny business.

The door opened and Knox poked his head inside, his face blooming into a smile when he saw her. "I thought you were going for a walk."

Aria shrugged under her covers. "I was, but then I realized I'd have to put on clothes."

And that smile turned wicked in one heartbeat. Knox slipped into the room and shut the door behind him. "Is that so?"

She nodded solemnly. "Clothes are the worst. I'm going to be naked from now on." She let the blanket drop off her shoulder, just a bit.

Knox groaned, low and sexy as sin. "All the time?" he asked. "You're going to cause a stir."

"Jealous?" She let the blanket slip completely off her shoulder so it just barely clung to the top of her breast. One deep breath and she'd be fully exposed.

She watched her dragon prowl closer. He wore loose pants that hung low on his hips and nothing else. "Incredibly. Do you like to tease, mate?

"Tease is one word." Aria let the blanket fall the rest of the way down to her waist and lifted her hands above her head in a stretch.

Knox's eyes went directly to her breasts and heated with that beautiful inner fire that never seemed to dim. He let out a growl before jumping on the bed. "Mine," he said, as he landed, placing both hands on her waist and dragging her body on top of his. "Fucking mine, always."

"Never forget that I'm the one who stole you." Her voice hitched on a moan as he spread her thighs to make more room for him. Her nakedness rubbed against his fabric-covered length, but that was a situation she could remedy. "I don't share."

Knox jerked the blanket completely away from her, his rough fingers leaving trails of heat over her skin until she was burning from head to toe with desire. "Never," he vowed. "You're everything, my mate." He sealed the vow with a heated kiss, teeth teasing her bottom lip until she writhed above him, grinding herself against him, seeking relief from the delicious torture that only Knox knew how to deliver.

When his mouth finally broke away from hers, she felt dizzy with pleasure and anticipation, every nerve ending standing on end. She gasped for air as Knox flipped her onto her back and braced himself above her, his massive biceps flexing as he stared down at her with those fiery eyes. "What's the magic word?"

"Now," she breathed, arching her hips, wrapping her legs around him and pressing herself against him as she sucked his bottom lip between her teeth.

The beast had the audacity to laugh as he kissed her again, but it was a desperate, frantic thing as he reached down to jerk at the string holding up his pants. "Impatient little human," he groaned.

Aria twisted and bucked, wiggling her way down his body and making her own demands with her tongue and lips. Knox let out a shout that turned into a strangled groan as she worked his cock free of its confines and wrapped her hand around his throbbing shaft. "Mate," he groaned as she lowered her mouth to taste him, the flavor of him exploding on her tongue and making her crave him even more. She sucked him into her mouth, watching that look of bliss and agony twist his features. Knox dropped his head back and let out a ragged cry. "Fuck, your mouth. Damnit."

But he wasn't done. She knew that. And she wanted him even wilder. She wanted him out of his mind with need, just like she was. They had forever. There would be plenty of time for slow, luxurious lovemaking. She needed him hard and fast, she needed his strength, his possessiveness. She needed to know that she could drive him insane, just as he did her.

Knox pulled back and drew in a couple of harsh breaths as she licked and nuzzled, not even trying to hide her satisfied smile. "Minx," he growled as he yanked her back up to the top of the bed. She wasn't even on her back before he'd pushed his way between her thighs.

"Oh!" she shouted as his mouth came down on her aching sex, his tongue finding that center of her need and stroking with masterful pressure and speed. Her hips arched up against him, and she fisted the sheets beneath her, her entire world narrowing to the building wave of pure sensation that only Knox could coax out of her. "More, please," she cried out, not even aware of what she was begging for, only knowing that Knox could give it to her.

"Yes, mate," he growled, the vibration of his words against her core nearly sending her tumbling over the edge, but somehow not quite enough.

"Knox!" She needed, and he gave. With a feral snarl, he shoved two fingers inside her wet, swollen folds, working her tender flesh until she was shivering and shaking in his grasp. "Please," she demanded, but before she could take another breath, she was flying. Knox pressed his mouth over her, sucking on her sensitive nub as her climax thundered through her. She clenched around him, but the orgasm showed no sign of abating, and she shuddered from head to toe, crying out as another rush of need cascaded over her, one more powerful than the last.

The world disappeared. She could barely hear Knox's soothing murmur as she came apart, breaking free into the most perfect kind of oblivion.

By the time she came to, Knox was settled over her, kissing her slowly and deeply as he braced himself on trembling arms, his cock poised at her entrance.

"I've got you," he whispered as he gently rocked against her.

Aria opened herself to him, her legs wide, her heart even wider. "I'm all yours."

He slipped into her warmth, inch by inch, until they were as close as two beings could be. Knox pressed his forehead against hers, breathing with her as they moved together, each stroke of his body within hers bringing them to new heights.

"My Aria," he murmured, as he drove deeper, his eyes meeting hers. Some of those tears she'd never admit to shedding threatened, but maybe it was just sweat.

She clutched at him, hungry for a kiss as his body took her deep. His lips crashed down on hers, their tongues tangled together in a wild rhythm as Knox drove into her, once, twice, again. He let out a roar that was swallowed by her mouth, and she followed him into bliss as he shuddered his release inside her. They stayed that way, wrapped together as tightly as possible as the waves of sensation rippled through them.

"Not bad for a warm up," Aria huffed out once she could finally manage to string two words together.

Knox's low, rumbling laugh vibrated against her as he wrapped an arm tight around her and held her close.

EPILOGUE

One month later

Soren still kind of hated her. He especially hated that she was in his house, at his dining room table, and eating the food prepared by his chef. Maze kept trying to slip her excess vegetables to the small yappy pet that kept jumping onto her chair, and every time she got caught, she'd get this longsuffering look on her face that made Aria bite her lip to keep from laughing.

Soren might not like her, but he'd accepted her. More or less.

Knox had made it clear from day one. If any of his family didn't like the woman he'd taken as a mate, they were welcome to get out of his life for good.

Being loved was... strange.

She still woke up some days worried she'd have to run. There was that restless urge that would always be at the back of her mind, warning her that the authorities were on the way and she had to get out *now*. Then she'd feel the warmth of Knox's body and snuggle into his side, reminded very firmly that she was *very* close to the authorities and she no longer had anything to fear.

As far as she knew, Ragnar was long gone. He'd disappeared into the hands of Imperium justice, and there was no escaping that. Anything he told them would seem like nothing more than the frantic rantings of a criminal desperate for clemency. It wasn't satisfying. It wasn't morally pure. But Aria would take the safety any day.

A wet plop of something green landed on the side of her skirt, and Mazy made a distressed sound. Aria saw the empty fork in the girl's hand and the begging pet at her chair and realized what happened.

With skills that had been honed over decades of thievery, Aria flicked her wrist to let the green stuff fall to the floor, where it was promptly gobbled up, then she winked at Mazy and went back to eating as if nothing had happened.

Mazy's mom covered her mouth with a napkin to hide her smile as the child started giggling. Even Soren's expression softened ever so slightly.

When she glanced over at Knox, he was looking at her as if she'd just plucked the sun out of the sky and offered it to him. All for a green bean caper.

She reached over and plucked a sliver of cheese off of Knox's plate and popped it into her mouth, offering him a grin. There was no completely taking the thief out of the girl.

But maybe, just maybe, there was a life beyond anything she'd ever dreamed of. She couldn't wait to figure out what came next.

WANT JUST ONE MORE SCENE?

Get a free bonus scene featuring Knox & Aria delivered straight to your inbox!
Sign up now: https://katerudolph.net/index.php/knox-bonus-sign-up/

Thank you for reading Knox! The series continues with *Flint*.

Read now!: https://shop.katerudolph.net/products/
flint

Ready to give audio a try? Get a free audiobook here!
https://katerudolph.net/index.php/free-audiobook

WHAT TO READ NEXT: CRUX

Prince Crux is in a bind.

When the Dragon King commands Crux find a mate, his days of carefree bachelorhood are over. One trip to a psychic matchmaker and he's on the path to his destiny. But it all comes screeching to a halt when he meets a human woman who lights his inner fire and makes him yearn.

She's got a pair of roller skates and an attitude.

Courtney is supposed to be putting the shambles of her life back together. Getting abducted by aliens isn't part of the plan. Neither is getting rescued by a scorchingly hot dragon that makes her think of an impossible future. But they have no chance together if they can't first escape a planet full of monsters intent on their destruction.

PREVIEW CRUX

Courtney Lamb's feet were heavy, and she had the headache to end all headaches. She curled into herself on one side, trying to scrunch up into a ball, but her feet dragged along the floor and noise echoed off the metal walls around her.

She was still wearing her roller skates.

How? She always took them off before leaving work. She couldn't exactly drive with wheels on her feet. And yet, as she turned over and pulled her legs in, they slipped on the cold metal floor.

Where was she? This wasn't the root beer stand she worked at, nor was it the creepy, decrepit steel barn that sat on the very edge of the restaurant property. She looked around, squinting in the dim light and trying to get her bearings.

It was industrial, but the room was small. Steel walls. No windows. And a weird echo-y noise in the distance that might have been an air conditioner.

She didn't see a door.

Courtney scrambled to her knees before realizing she wasn't going to get far with roller skates on her feet. She shucked the skates off and wiggled her toes in her sweaty socks before tying the laces together. No matter what was going on, she didn't want to lose her skates.

They were expensive. And one of the few nice things she had left.

There was a shriek down the hall, or at least, Courtney assumed there was a hall, and she flinched.

What the hell was going on?

Had she been kidnapped? Was she being trafficked? She'd seen plenty of Facebook posts talking about the perils of being a woman in America, but most of it seemed like a bunch of bullshit. People didn't *actually* hide under cars to slit the Achilles tendons of the unsuspecting.

Right?

She ran a hand down the back of her leg, as if to assure herself that she was intact. Obviously she was. Other than the headache, she wasn't hurt.

She was just confused.

And in trouble.

She wanted to call for help, but a second scream from somewhere in the building made her throat freeze up. No, she didn't want to call attention to herself.

With her skate laces tied together, she was able to sling her skates over her shoulder and get to her feet. The room seemed even tinier when she was standing up. Was she a prisoner? Why?

Her mom was going to kill her when she found out.

Of course, Courtney hadn't spoken to her mother in months, and now was not the time to think about how this would impact her mother's career. She was in the middle of an abduction, she had to care about herself.

She stroked the top of her skate, half for comfort, half to remind herself that it was sturdy and could probably be used as some kind of weapon.

She was wearing the thick leggings and short sleeve red tunic that made up her work uniform, though her name badge must have fallen off somewhere. That furthered Courtney's theory that she'd been taken from work.

She couldn't remember clocking out. She

wracked her brain, but the last thing she remembered was telling her co-worker, Sarah, that she didn't have any plans for the weekend. The same as every weekend these days.

That wasn't what she should be feeling bad about at the moment.

Was Sarah a trafficker? Had she waited to strike until Courtney was at her most vulnerable?

No. That was ridiculous. Sarah was a college student trying to make ends meet. She wasn't sinister.

Where was the freaking door?

Courtney whirled around, but she still didn't see anything that looked like it would let her out of the room. She was in a metal tomb and she couldn't escape.

Her breaths came faster and faster, and black spots danced in front of her eyes.

No. No. Now was not the time for a panic attack.

She hadn't had one in months, and she didn't want them to restart. They sucked.

And so did her whole situation.

"Think of the good things," she commanded herself. There weren't many. But she had to number them off. "I'm in my regular clothes. My skates are fine. I'm not hurt." She ran out of optimism after that. Any other "good" news sounded like asking for trouble, and Courtney wasn't interested in that.

She ran her hands over the metal walls, looking for a seam that might reveal a hidden door. There had to be something. She had been put in the room, so there had to be a way to get her out of it. She looked up, wondering if she'd somehow been lowered in, but the ceiling was too high to make out any fine detail in the dim light.

Where was the light even coming from?

There wasn't a ceiling light. She didn't see lights in the floor. There was just a faint, pale blue glow all around her that allowed her to see.

It was another good thing, and Courtney decided not to question it.

She had her skates, but she wished she had a skate tool. That fancy little wrench might have helped her pry an invisible door open. But her skate tool and spare wheels were in her bag at work. Along with her cell phone, a bit of cash, and her car keys. She had no way to contact anyone for help.

And *there* was the hyperventilation.

She tried to control her breathing, but the walls felt like they were closing in. She heard footsteps coming her way and shrank back as far away from the sound as she could. The room was maybe six feet wide. She couldn't shrink back much.

A brave woman would have done something. Courtney *wished* she was brave. But she couldn't think and she wanted to live. She was pretty sure brave people died quicker than cowards.

The wall opposite her glowed a faint yellow, and a rectangle formed before sliding to one side, the invisible door revealing itself. A brave woman would have charged.

Instead, Courtney watched a monster step inside.

It—and it was clearly an *it*, not a person—was some kind of *creature*. Over eight feet tall, antennae coming out of its head, and sinister purple skin that was covered in a faint slime. It wore clothes over most of its body, but its arms were exposed, and scars or tattoos or something covered it.

One of its hands wasn't a hand at all. Instead, it came to a fine point and had an edge that made it look like a sword.

It looked like something out of *Star Trek*.

And she was wearing a red shirt.

Shit.

It wore pants, but judging by the giant bulge right where his dick should be, he didn't plan on wearing them for long. And she didn't want to find out if his dick was a knife too.

Working by instinct, not pausing to think, Courtney grabbed onto one of her skates and swung, sending the other one flying at the monster's head. He didn't expect it, and the wheels, metal plate, and carbon fiber boot were enough to send him slumping to the ground.

Oh god, was he dead? Had she broken her skate?

Courtney flailed for a moment and cut off the horrible noise that tried to escape her throat. She checked her skate first. Except for a bit of slime and something that might have been monster blood, it seemed fine.

Good.

She didn't know how to check for a pulse on a monster. She didn't know if she wanted him to be dead or alive.

Oh god. What was she going to do?

She had to run.

She stepped around the monster and dove through the door, just in case it tried to close. The hallway was narrow and lit up by the same ambient blue light as her cell. She chose a direction and ran, unsure if it was correct but refusing to hesitate.

She stumbled when she passed a window.

Courtney came to a halt and looked outside.

She expected a city. Maybe some trees. *Something*.

Instead, she saw the black of space.

Outer space.

She wasn't in a warehouse. She was on a space ship, and they were hovering above some planet that didn't look like Earth.

How was she going to get home?

She was trying to think, then something impacted the ship, and Courtney stumbled as the lights went out and all of her senses went haywire.

JOIN THE CELESTIAL HEARTS CLUB

Hey there, **wonderful reader! Are you ready to take our relationship to the next level?**

By becoming a member of the Celestial Hearts Club, you'll get access to:

- early access to chapters from books before they're published
- exclusive short stories - at least one a month!
- sneak peeks that will make your heart skip a beat

Plus, you'll be directly contributing to the creation of more epic love stories and heart pounding space adventures.

Are you ready to hop on board and support the creation of more out-of-this-world romance?

Check it out!

https://katerudolph.net/celestialheartsclub

INTERGALACTIC DATING AGENCY

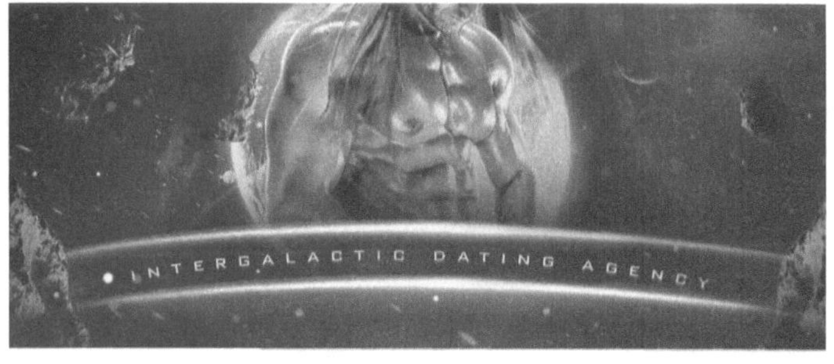

LOOKING for love that's out of this world? These strong, smart, sexy aliens are seeking mates from the Milky Way. Just hop onboard with your local Intergalactic Dating Agency. Join our group of authors as we explore the friendly skies and beyond with trilogies of cosmic craving, astral adventure, and otherworldly lovers. Warning: abductions may or may not be included!

Guarded by the Shifter

Werewolf. Bodyguard. Mate.
The origins of these shifters are shrouded in mystery, but they're determined to protect their mates from any harm that comes their way.
Also available in audio!
Hunting Season
On the Prowl
Stalking Magic
Hungry for the Wolf
Wolf Cursed (novella)
Wolf's Temptation

Stealing the Alpha

The thief takes what she wants, but the alpha keeps what's his...
Join shifter thief Mel as she clashes with lion alpha Luke in an explosive trilogy of two opposites who can't keep away from one another.
Also available in audio!
The Alpha Heist

Entangled with the Thief
In the Alpha's Bed

———

Alien Mates: Planet Exile

Guerran is no place for pretty human women. But these alien heroes will protect their mates!
Also available in audio!

Exile's Hunter
Exile's Adored

———

Zulir Warrior Mates

Kidnapped humans. Alien Warriors. Electric wings.
The Zulir Warrior Mates series brings you human heroines and heroes abducted from Earth who find love – and wings! – with the alien warriors who rescue them.
Also available in audio!

Synnr's Saint

Synnr's Hope

Synnr's Spark

Synnr's Kiss

Synnr's Ride

Mated to the Alien

Fated Mate Alien Romance

Detyens are doomed to die young if they don't find their fated mates.

Follow along as these mated pairs fight off aliens, corrupt dictators, prejudiced humans, pirates, and more! The books can be read or listened to in any order, though some characters show up in multiple stories.

Select books available in audio.

Pick a book and jump into the action today!

Ruwen

Tyral

Stoan

Cyborg

Krayter

Kayleb

Shayn

Braxtyn

Doryan

Dekon

———

Detyen Warriors

Detya was destroyed a hundred years ago. These doomed warriors are out to find justice... and their mates.

The Detyen Warriors series brings you kick butt heroines, alpha alien heroes, fated mates, and relationships strong enough to span the galaxy!

The entire series is also available in audio!

Soulless

Ruthless

Heartless

Faultless

Endless

———

Alien Holiday Romance

Christmas... in space????
These alien holiday romances look beyond Earth's
winter holidays and ring in the season across the
galaxy!
Select titles available in audio.
Snowed in with the Alien Beast
The Alien's Winter Gift
The Alien Reindeer's Wild Ride
Trapped with her Alien Mate

Alien Outlaws

**Outlaws, schemes, and love... it's all there in the
Alien Outlaws series...**

Andie Munster is sick of life on Ixilta, the planet she
got dumped on after being abducted from Earth six
years ago. And when the mysterious and dangerous
Xandr shows up looking for a way off the planet,
she's half-prisoner, half-co-conspirator in a wild
rush to escape.

Rogue Alien's Escape
Rogue Alien's Woman
Rogue Alien's Secret
Rogue Alien's Legacy

Find more by Kate Rudolph at www.
katerudolph.net

ABOUT KATE RUDOLPH

KATE RUDOLPH IS a paranormal and sci-fi romance writer who lives in Indiana. She loves writing about kick butt heroines and the steamy heroes who love them. She's been devouring romance novels since she was too young to be reading them and had to hide her books so no one would take them away. She couldn't imagine a better job in this world than writing romances and sharing them with her fellow readers.

If you enjoyed this story, please consider leaving a review.